Ellen
Tebbits

OTHER YEARLING BOOKS YOU WILL ENJOY:

Henry Huggins, BEVERLY CLEARY
Beezus and Ramona, BEVERLY CLEARY
Ramona and Her Father, BEVERLY CLEARY
Freddy the Detective, WALTER R. BROOKS
How to Eat Fried Worms, THOMAS ROCKWELL
Chocolate Fever, ROBERT KIMMEL SMITH
Henry Reed's Big Show, KEITH ROBERTSON
The Enormous Egg, OLIVER BUTTERWORTH
Mr. Popper's Penguins, RICHARD AND FLORENCE ATWATER
Freckle Juice, JUDY BLUME

YEARLING BOOKS are designed especially to entertain and en-
lighten young people. The finest available books for children
have been selected under the direction of Charles F. Reasoner,
Professor of Elementary Education, New York University.

For a complete listing of all Yearling titles, write to Education
Sales Department, Dell Publishing Co., Inc., 1 Dag Hammarskjold Plaza, New York, New York 10017.

Ellen Tebbits

By BEVERLY CLEARY

Illustrated by Louis Darling

A YEARLING BOOK

A YEARLING BOOK
Published by
Dell Publishing Co., Inc.
1 Dag Hammarskjold Plaza
New York, New York 10017

Yearling ® TM 913705, Dell Publishing Co., Inc.

ISBN: 440-2299-7

Reprinted by arrangement with
William Morrow & Company, New York

Printed in the United States of America
Fourth Dell Printing—December 1981

Book Club Edition

Contents

CHAPTER ONE

Ellen's Secret

ELLEN TEBBITS was in a hurry. As she ran down Tillamook Street with her ballet slippers tucked under her arm, she did not even stop to scuff through the autumn leaves on the sidewalk. The reason Ellen was in a hurry was a secret she would never, never tell.

Ellen was a thin little girl, with dark hair and brown eyes. She wore bands on her teeth, and her hair was scraggly on the left side of her face, because she spent so much time reading and twisting a lock of hair around her finger as she read. She had no brothers or sisters and, since Nancy Jane had moved away from next door, there was no one her own age living on Tillamook Street.

So she had no really best friend. She did not even have a dog or cat to play with, because her mother said animals tracked in mud and left hair on the furniture.

Of course Ellen had lots of friends at school, but that was not the same as having a best friend who lived in the same neighborhood and could come over to play after school and on Saturdays. Today, however, Ellen was almost glad she did not have a best friend, because best friends do not have secrets from one another. She was sure she would rather be lonely the rest of her life than share the secret of why she had to get to her dancing class before any of the other girls.

The Spofford School of the Dance was upstairs over the Payless Drugstore. When Ellen came to the entrance at the side of the building, she paused to look anxiously up and down the street. Then, relieved that she saw no one she knew, she scampered up the long flight of steps as fast as she could run. There was not a minute to waste.

She pushed open the door and looked quickly around the big, bare room. Maybe her plan was really going to work after all. She was the first pupil to arrive.

Ellen's teacher, Valerie Todd Spofford, was looking at some music with Mrs. Adams, the accompanist, at the piano in the corner of the room.

She was really Mrs. John Spofford and had a son named Otis, who was in Ellen's room at school. Because she taught dancing, people did not call her Mrs. John Spofford. They called her by her full name, Valerie Todd Spofford.

"Good afternoon, Ellen," she said. "You're early."

"Good afternoon, Mrs. Spofford," answered Ellen, and hurried past the long mirrors that covered one wall.

When Ellen opened the dressing-room door, she made a terrible discovery. Someone was in the dressing room ahead of her.

Austine Allen was sitting on a bench lacing her ballet slippers. Austine was a new girl, both in the dancing class and in Ellen's room at school. Ellen knew she had just come from California, because she mentioned it so often. She thought the new girl looked good-natured and untidy, but she really had not paid much attention to her.

"Oh," said Ellen. "Hello. I didn't know anyone was here."

"I guess I'm early," said Austine and then added, "but so are you."

The girls looked at each other. Ellen noticed that Austine had already changed into the required costume of the Spofford School of the Dance. This was a short full skirt of tulle gathered onto a sateen top that had straps over the shoulders. Austine looked chubby in her green costume.

Neither girl spoke. Oh, why doesn't she leave, thought Ellen desperately. Maybe if I wait long enough she'll go into the other room. Ellen removed her jacket as slowly as she could. No, I can't wait. The others will be here any minute.

"This is a silly costume we have to wear," said Austine. "When I took ballet lessons in California we always wore shorts and T shirts."

"Well, I think it's pretty," said Ellen, as she took her pink costume from the rack along the wall. Why don't you go away, she thought. She said, "It's almost like real ballerinas wear. When I'm wearing it, I pretend I'm a real dancer."

Austine stood up. "Not even real ballerinas

practice in full skirts like these. They wear leotards. In California . . ."

"Well, I think leotards are ugly," interrupted Ellen, who was glad she knew that leotards were long tight-fitting garments. "They look just like long underwear and I wouldn't wear one for anything. I like our dresses better."

"I don't," said Austine flatly. "I don't even like dancing lessons. At least in California . . ."

"I don't care what anybody does in California," said Ellen crossly. "I'm tired of hearing you talk about California and so is everyone at school. So there! If you think California is so wonderful, why don't you go back there?"

For a second Austine looked hurt. Ellen almost thought she was going to cry. Instead she made a face. "All right for you!" she said, and flounced out of the dressing room, leaving her clothes in an untidy heap on the bench.

Instantly Ellen was sorry. What a terrible thing to say to a new girl! What if she herself were a new girl and someone had said that to her? How would she have felt? She hadn't really meant to be rude, but somehow it had slipped out. She was so anxious to have Austine leave that she had not thought about what she was saying.

But now that Austine was gone and Ellen was alone, there was not a moment to waste, not even in feeling sorry for what she had done. Feverishly she unbuttoned her sweater. She was starting to unfasten her dress when she heard some of the girls coming through the classroom.

Frantically Ellen looked around the dressing room for a place to hide. She darted behind the costume rack. No, that wouldn't do. The girls might see her when they took down their costumes.

Snatching her pink dancing dress from the bench, Ellen dashed across the room and into the janitor's broom closet, just as the girls came into the room.

If only there were some way of locking the closet door from the inside! Ellen stood silent and rigid. When no one came near the door, she relaxed enough to look around by the light of the window high in the closet. She could see brooms, a mop and buckets, and a gunny sack full of sweeping compound.

Careful not to knock over the brooms and buckets, she leaned against the door to listen. She could hear Linda and Janet and Barbara. Then she heard Betsy come in and, after a few minutes, Amelia and Joanne. Ellen counted them off on her fingers. Yes, they were all there.

Trying to move carefully so she wouldn't bump into anything, she took off first her starched plaid dress and then her slip. But she was so nervous that she knocked over a broom. She stood terrified and motionless until she realized that the girls were chattering so noisily they did not hear the thud. If one of the girls had opened the door at that moment, they all would have learned her terrible secret.

Ellen was wearing woolen underwear.

She was wearing a high-necked union suit that buttoned down the front and across the back. It did have short sleeves and short legs, so it could

have been worse. Ellen didn't know what she would have done if her mother had made her wear long underwear.

With trembling fingers she slipped her arms out of the despised garment, rolled it as flat as she could down to her waist, and pulled the elastic of her panties over the bulge. Quickly she slipped into her costume.

"I wonder where Ellen is," she heard someone ask.

"I don't know," someone answered. "Maybe she isn't coming today."

Ellen was limp with relief. She was safely in her costume. No one had seen her in her underwear. Nobody could tease her and tell her she was old-fashioned because, besides being the only girl in the third grade who had to wear winter underwear, she was the only girl in the whole school who did.

She took off her shoes and socks, laced her slippers, and waited, shivering, until all the girls left the dressing room. Then she slipped out of the closet and, after piling her clothes neatly on a bench, joined the others in the classroom.

A couple of girls were running and sliding the length of the room, and others were practicing at the exercise bar that was built along the mirror-covered wall. All the girls stopped when Ellen appeared.

"Well, where did you come from?" asked Linda Mulford.

"The dressing room," answered Ellen briefly, as she took hold of the bar and began to practice a circular movement of one leg that Mrs. Spofford called a *rond de jambe*. She felt uncomfortable, because all the girls were looking at her. She hoped the bulge around her middle did not show.

"I didn't see you," said Amelia.

Ellen pretended to be so interested in rotating her leg that she didn't hear. If she kept moving, maybe no one would notice the goose flesh on her bare shoulders.

"I didn't see you either," said Joanne. "Where were you?"

"Oh, I was there," said Ellen vaguely. "You just didn't see me."

She twirled her leg faster. Then she looked in the mirror and saw Austine watching her. Ellen felt sorrier than ever for what she had said, because Austine looked so unhappy. She was practicing alone at the end of the bar and none of the other girls were talking to her.

Valerie Todd Spofford walked to the center of the room. "All right, girls," she said. "Let's get in line in front of the mirror."

The girls stood several feet apart, in a row. Ellen was careful not to stand near Austine, who, she could tell by looking in the mirror, remained at the end of the line.

Valerie Todd Spofford stood in front of the girls with her back to the mirror. "Now, girls, we will go through the five positions of the ballet. Remember, ballet dancing is based on these positions. To be good dancers we must learn them perfectly. First position." She stood with her heels together and her toes turned out, and held her arms slightly out from her sides. The girls imitated her as she looked critically up and down the line.

"Knees together, Joanne," she corrected. "Turn your toes farther out, Amelia. That's right, Linda. Splendid!"

Ellen was careful to do everything exactly right, because she did not want Mrs. Spofford to call attention to her. The five positions of the ballet were easy for her, because she practiced them every night before she went to bed. Now, as she pointed her toes and held out her arms, she thought more and more about what she had said to Austine. What a terrible person she was to make a new girl unhappy! Again she looked in the mirror at Austine and thought how lonely she looked, standing at the end of the line a little apart from the other girls.

Ellen knew what it felt like to be lonely, because she had been lonely herself since Nancy Jane had moved away. Maybe Austine sat on her front steps and wished she had someone to play with. Maybe she hoped someone in the dancing class would ask her to come over after school. The very least Ellen could do was to be friendly. She made up her mind to tell Austine she was sorry the first chance she had.

"Fourth position," said Mrs. Spofford. "No, Janet. We do not raise both arms over our head in the fourth position." She walked over to Janet and arranged her arms so that one was circled over her head and the other was held out from her side.

Here was Ellen's chance! When she saw that Valerie Todd Spofford was not watching the whole class, she slipped out of her place in line, darted behind several of the girls, and stepped into line beside Austine, where she quickly assumed a perfect fourth position.

"Austine," she whispered, "I'm sorry I said what I did. I really didn't mean it. Honestly, I didn't."

"Ellen," said Mrs. Spofford sharply, "have you forgotten that we do not whisper during our dancing lesson?"

"No, Mrs. Spofford," said Ellen.

"All right, girls. Fourth position again!"

Ellen arranged her arms and legs in the correct position once more. Mrs. Spofford was watching, so Ellen could not catch Austine's eye in the mirror. Had Austine forgiven her? She couldn't tell, but she hoped so. The more she thought about the lonely new girl, the more she wanted her for a friend.

It was not until Valerie Todd Spofford asked the girls to assume the fifth position that Ellen felt her underwear slip. Oh my, she thought, what am I going to do now? How can I hold it up when I have to raise my hands over my head? Carefully she arranged her feet and lifted her arms to form a circle. The underwear slid alarmingly.

As she stood in the fifth position, Ellen heard someone running up the long flight of stairs. When the footsteps neared the classroom, she heard a jingling sound. Oh dear, thought Ellen. That sound could mean only one person—Otis Spofford.

Most of the boys and many of the girls at school owned a cowboy hat or neckerchief. Several even had boots, but Otis was the only one who owned a pair of real spurs that jingled when he walked.

Now he burst into the room, the spurs on his tennis shoes clinking against the hardwood floor. "Hey, Mom," he demanded, "can I have a dime?"

"Otis dear, you are interrupting the lesson," answered his mother, as the girls lowered their arms and turned to look at him. "All right, girls, let us do the fifth position again."

Ellen carefully arranged her feet so that the heel of one foot touched the toe of the other foot. Then, just before she raised her arms to form a circle over her head, she gave her underwear a quick hitch.

Looking into the mirror to see if the bulge showed, she saw that Otis was standing directly behind her. He too arranged his feet, made a hitching motion, and raised his arms. At the same time he blew a huge bubble with his gum.

Ellen was horrified. What if Otis guessed her trouble! She was even more horrified when she felt her underwear slipping again. Quickly she put her hand on her hip.

Otis put his hand on his hip.

Ellen raised her arm again. The underwear slid still more.

Otis raised his arm again and blew another bubble.

"Now, girls, we will go through the positions once more. First position," said Mrs. Spofford.

Ellen set her heels together and turned her toes out. She gave her sliding underwear a discreet tug before she held her arms out from her sides.

Otis turned his toes out, tugged, and held his arms out from his sides.

Ellen turned and whispered fiercely, "Otis Spofford! You go away!"

Otis looked cross-eyed at Ellen and blew another bubble with his gum.

"Ellen Tebbits," said Mrs. Spofford, "I have already spoken to you about whispering in class."

"I'm sorry, Mrs. Spofford," replied Ellen.

"Second position," said Mrs. Spofford.

Ellen had been pressing her knees tightly together to keep her underwear from slipping. Now she grasped it again, at the same time trying to feel through her costume for the elastic of her panties, and yanked it into place. She could tell that her underwear had come unrolled. Then she held her arms out from her sides.

Miserable because she could do nothing to stop Otis, Ellen watched him in the mirror. He copied her movements exactly.

By this time all the girls were watching Ellen and Otis in the mirror. Ellen knew they could not help seeing how thick she was around the middle.

"Third position," said Mrs. Spofford.

Ellen was determined not to tug at her underwear again. Surely it could not fall any farther. She moved as carefully as she could, but once more the underwear slid. Ellen had to grab it and pull it into place.

This time the girls giggled when Otis imitated her. Ellen swallowed and blinked her eyes to keep from crying. Why did Otis have to pick on her? Why couldn't he tease someone else?

Then, to her amazement, Austine spoke out

loud. "Otis Spofford! You stop bothering us," she said loudly.

Everyone was startled, because no one ever talked out loud during a ballet lesson. The girls stopped looking at Ellen and stared at Austine. Ellen gave her underwear a good hard tug while no one was watching. Was Austine really trying to keep Otis from teasing her? If only Ellen knew for sure.

"I'm sorry, Mrs. Spofford," said Austine. "Otis is bothering me so I can't do the steps right."

"Otis dear," said Mrs. Spofford, "you know Mother doesn't like her boy to come into the studio while she is giving a lesson."

"Can I have a dime?" asked Otis.

"Mother is busy now, Otis," said Valerie Todd Spofford. "All right, girls. Let's do our exercises at the bar."

Otis clinked across the floor to the piano, where he leaned over the keyboard and amused himself by blowing bigger and bigger bubbles with his gum.

After the exercises at the bar, Mrs. Spofford had the girls practice the Dance of the Falling Leaves while Mrs. Adams played *Rhapsody of Autumn* on the piano and glared at Otis.

Every time Ellen leaped, her underwear slipped. After each leap she had to clutch it and pull it into place. In the mirror she could see that she looked more and more bulgy. Leap and clutch, leap and clutch. Ellen thought they would never finish being falling leaves.

When Mrs. Adams came to the end of *Rhapsody of Autumn,* Otis added to the tune by picking out "Shave and a haircut—six bits" on the bass keys of the piano. Mrs. Adams was annoyed, but Otis looked pleased when the girls giggled. Ellen was glad he had found someone else to tease.

Mrs. Spofford did not pay any attention to Otis. "Once more, girls," she said.

Then it was leap and clutch, leap and clutch again. Ellen stayed as far away from Otis as she could and hoped he would continue to bother Mrs. Adams.

Finally Valerie Todd Spofford clapped her hands for attention. "Ellen Tebbits," she said. "I think you have forgotten. Falling leaves do not put their hands on their hips. They flutter their arms slowly and gracefully." She fluttered her arms slowly and gracefully.

"Yes, Mrs. Spofford," said Ellen miserably. Usually her dancing was praised.

"Try to watch the way Linda dances and think of falling leaves. Think what falling leaves feel like."

"Yes, Mrs. Spofford," answered Ellen, telling herself glumly that she was too busy thinking about falling underwear to think about falling leaves. She noticed Barbara glance at her waistline and whisper something to Amelia.

"All right, Mrs. Adams. We will take it from *tum tum te tum.*" Mrs. Spofford hummed a few bars of *Rhapsody of Autumn.*

The girls leaped and fluttered their arms. By making short awkward leaps, Ellen managed not to clutch her underwear. Then to Ellen's horror,

Otis suddenly bounded onto the floor with a loud jangle of spurs. Leaping and clutching, he began to dance beside Ellen. But Otis did not come down lightly on his toes like a falling leaf. He landed with a flat-footed thud. His spurs made more noise that way.

The girls began to snicker. Ellen stopped dancing, but Otis went on leaping and clutching. She could see that he knew the Dance of the Falling Leaves as well as she did. I wish he would trip on his spurs, she thought crossly.

Then Ellen noticed Austine lengthen her leaps. She could not help thinking that Austine did not look a bit like a falling leaf. She was out of breath and she did not flutter gracefully. She flapped.

When Austine caught up with Otis, who was making an extra-long leap, she suddenly sprang sideways. They collided in mid-air and both sat down hard on the slippery floor.

"Ouch," said Austine loudly, as everyone stopped dancing. "Mrs. Spofford, Otis bumped into me."

"I did not," said Otis. "You jumped in front of me."

"Well, you weren't supposed to be there," said Austine, as she stood up and rubbed herself "Was he, Mrs. Spofford?"

"Otis, run along and play like a good boy," said Valerie Todd Spofford.

"Can I have a dime if I go?" asked Otis, untangling his spurs and standing up.

"All right, just this once." Mrs. Spofford took a dime from her purse on the piano and handed it to her son. Otis made a face at the girls and ran out of the room, the jingle of his spurs growing fainter as he ran down the steps. Ellen sighed with relief

"Once more, girls," said Valerie Todd Spofford.

Austine smiled triumphantly at Ellen, who gratefully returned her smile. Austine had bumped into Otis on purpose! Ellen knew now for sure that Austine had forgiven her and wanted to be friends. She was very glad, but she began to worry about getting into the broom closet without being seen by the other girls. And what about Austine? Now that they were friendly, she would expect Ellen to talk to her in the dressing room. The lesson certainly could not last much longer, so Ellen danced her way nearer the dressing-room door.

Finally Mrs. Spofford clapped her hands. "Girls, before I dismiss the class I have a little announcement to make," she said. "Next week members of all my classes are going to give a program for the soldiers and sailors in the Veterans Hospital. I should like to have some of you girls put on your little Dance of the Falling Leaves. It is such a sweet dance and it is so appropriate for this time of year, I am sure the men will enjoy it. Those of you who think your mothers will let you go, please give me your names before you leave."

Ellen thought it would be wonderful to dance on a real stage with a real live audience just like a grown-up ballerina. She knew she would dance so beautifully that she would be called back for

encore after encore. Eagerly she crowded up to
Mrs. Spofford with the rest of the girls.

Then she remembered her underwear. She
wanted so much to dance at the Veterans Hospital
that she was almost willing to risk having the girls
find out about her underwear. Almost, but not
quite. She wiggled out of the group of girls, ran
across the polished floor, and darted into the
empty dressing room. Snatching her street clothes
from the bench, she flung open the door of the
broom closet. Then she stopped, astounded at
what she saw.

Austine Allen was already in the broom closet.

Ellen could not believe her eyes. Austine was
wearing woolen underwear.

"Shut the door!" ordered Austine.

Ellen stood with her mouth open. Austine's
high-necked underwear buttoned down the front
and across the back just like hers.

"Didn't you hear me? Shut the door!"

"Do you—do you wear woolen underwear, too?"
asked Ellen, still not believing what she saw.

"Shut the door," ordered Austine for the third time, as she yanked her slip over her head. She poked her head through the slip and said crossly, "Yes, I do."

By now Ellen had her wits about her. She joined Austine in the broom closet and closed the door. "And I thought I was the only girl in the whole school who had to wear it," she said, and sat down on the bag of sweeping compound.

"And I thought I was the only one," said Austine, "until I watched you in the mirror. I sort of thought that was why you looked so bumpy around the waist."

"That old Otis Spofford makes me so mad," said Ellen. "Do you suppose he really guessed? I don't know what I'd have done if you hadn't spoken right out loud like you did." As she hastily stood up again and began to change her clothes, Ellen smiled at Austine. "Promise you won't tell anybody," she begged.

"I promise if you promise," said Austine. "My mother makes me wear the old stuff because she says it's so much colder here than it is in California."

"I promise," agreed Ellen. "Mother says I have to wear it because I'm thin and catch cold easily. I'd just die if anyone at school knew about it."

"Me too," said Austine.

"How did you keep yours from slipping?" asked Ellen.

"I brought a string and tied it around my waist. Sh-h-h. Here they come."

"We'll have to stay here until they go," whispered Ellen. Both girls dressed quickly and silently. Then, as they waited, they listened to the other girls chatter.

"Where are Austine and Ellen?" they heard Joanne say. "I didn't see them leave."

"I didn't either," said Linda, "and I just know Ellen wasn't in here before the lesson. I wonder where she came from."

"She couldn't have come from any place but here," said Barbara. "Say, where does that door go?"

"That's just the janitor's closet."

"I'll bet they're in there," said Linda, and flung open the door. "There you are!" she exclaimed triumphantly. "What are you doing in there?"

Ellen and Austine looked at each other and began to giggle.

"Oh, we were just hiding," said Austine.

"We just wanted to see if you would miss us," added Ellen. "Come on, Austine, let's go home." She wasn't going to give the others a chance to ask any more questions.

When they were out on the sidewalk, Austine asked timidly, "Do I really talk about California too much?"

Ellen was embarrassed. "Well, you do talk about it quite a lot, but I shouldn't have said anything. I guess I was just worried about someone finding out about my underwear."

"I suppose I do talk about California a lot," said Austine slowly, "but I miss it—all the kids I used to play with there and everything. Here it rains all the time, and I have to stay in the house a lot,

and anyway there isn't anyone in my block to play with."

"There isn't anyone in my block to play with, either. I live on Tillamook Street. Where do you live?"

"On Forty-first next to the house with the little gnomes in the front yard."

"I know where that is," exclaimed Ellen. "I like to walk past there and look at the gnomes. I like the one with the spade best."

"He's my favorite, too," agreed Austine. "Second best I like the one with the wheelbarrow."

Ellen thought a minute. "You live only two

blocks from my house. Just down the street and
around the corner."

"Do I?" Austine was delighted. "Maybe you
could come over sometime. Why don't you come
home with me now? My mother could phone your
mother."

"I'd love to. I'm sure Mother would let me if
your mother phones."

"And we can bake brownies," said Austine.

Ellen was impressed. "Do you know how to
bake brownies?"

"Sure. I bake them all the time. My brother eats
so many they don't last long at our house."

"I can make pudding out of a package," said Ellen, "but I can t do anything hard like brownies. There are eggs in brownies, aren t there?"

"Just two."

Ellen was even more impressed. "My mother let me break an egg once. I hit it on the edge of a bowl just like she does, but when I tried to break it in two, I stuck my thumbs into the yolk and messed it all up."

"I know what," said Austine. "You crack the nuts and I'll break the eggs and do the rest."

"Swell," agreed Ellen. "I'm good at cracking nuts."

The girls smiled at each other. "You know something?" said Ellen. "I don't mind this awful underwear half so much, now that I know I'm not the only one in school who has to wear it."

"Isn't it funny?" said Austine. "That's just the way I feel."

CHAPTER TWO

The Biennial
Beet

AT first Ellen thought everything about the third grade was going to be perfect. The nicest part of all was knowing Austine. She thought they were best friends, but she wasn't quite sure. Austine hadn't said anything about being best friends. But the two girls were always together at dancing class and at school, and they liked to play at each other's houses.

Austine liked to play at Ellen's house because the attic was full of such interesting things—old clothes for dressing up, a violin with half the strings missing, piles of magazines full of coupons to send away for free samples. The basement was an interesting place, too, and the girls spent one

rainy afternoon there blowing bubbles in a bucket
of soapsuds with an old tire pump. Austine had
never lived in a house with a basement or an attic
before she moved to Oregon. Anyway, her mother
believed in sending old things to the Goodwill
instead of keeping them in case they might come
in handy some day.

The rest of Ellen's house was nice, too, but in a different way. The furniture was polished, the floors shone, and everything was in perfect order. Austine always felt she should be on her very best behavior, so she wouldn't leave marks on the floor or knock over a vase. Mrs. Tebbits used her nicest dishes for serving cookies and tea made with lots of milk. That made Austine feel grown up.

Ellen liked to go to Austine's home because it was next door to the house with the gnomes on the lawn and because, although there was nothing in the Allens' attic but empty trunks and packing cases, the rest of the house was such a nice place to play. The furniture was old and comfortable, and there was nothing that could be easily broken. Best of all, Austine's mother did not mind the girls' making brownies in her kitchen. If they spilled cooky batter on the floor, she never said, "Oh dear, my clean floor!" Instead, she found a cloth for wiping up the batter. Ellen thought this was a nice way for a mother to be.

Next to having Austine for a friend, Ellen felt

that the best thing about the third grade was having Miss Joyce for her teacher. Miss Joyce was the nicest teacher in Rosemont School. She was never impatient and almost never cross. Besides, she was young and pretty and had curly hair.

Unlike other teachers, Miss Joyce never wore dark blouses and skirts or sensible shoes. She wore the prettiest clothes Ellen had ever seen. Ellen liked best of all a yellow woolen dress that made her think of sunshine on rainy winter days. With the yellow dress Miss Joyce always wore beautiful red shoes with high heels.

"Red and yellow, catch a fellow," Otis whispered whenever Miss Joyce wore the dress, but Ellen made up her mind that when she was grown up she was going to have a yellow dress and a pair of red shoes with teetery heels just like her teacher's.

But, much as Ellen loved Miss Joyce, she was not quite happy in Miss Joyce's room. Of course, Miss Joyce was always very nice to Ellen. She was patient with her mistakes in arithmetic and praised her reading, even when she mispronounced words. She always noticed when Ellen wore a new dress to school and told her how pretty she thought it was.

Just the same, as the days went by, Ellen became more and more certain that Miss Joyce did not like her as much as she liked the other boys and girls. Ellen was sure of this, because Miss Joyce never asked her to clap erasers.

Every day, just before afternoon recess, Miss Joyce named two children to collect all the blackboard erasers, take them outdoors, and beat the chalk dust out of them. Every day when it came time for Miss Joyce to select the children, Ellen was hopeful, but Miss Joyce always chose someone else. When the boys and girls went out for recess, Ellen would wait her turn at hopscotch and wistfully watch the lucky pair as they clapped erasers together and made chalk dust fly. If the erasers were extra dirty, they would make faces and turn their heads away as they beat out the dust. Sometimes they beat the erasers against the brick building. Ellen wanted more than anything to make chalk dust fly and to beat a white pattern on the red building.

Finally in November, when Austine had clapped erasers twice and Otis had clapped them three times, Ellen said to Austine, "If Miss Joyce really liked me, I just know she would choose me to clap the erasers."

"It's funny she's never picked you," agreed Austine, "but she sends you to the principal's office with notes and she never lets me go."

Ellen liked to be sent to the principal's office with notes. She liked having the long halls all to herself, with no hall monitors around to keep her from running and leaping. She did this very quietly on her toes, pretending she was a ballerina. It was fun, but it wasn't the same as clapping erasers.

Finally Ellen made up her mind that she would have to do something special to please Miss Joyce. She didn't know what it would be, but it would have to be something Miss Joyce couldn't help noticing.

One day Miss Joyce sent the class to the board to review arithmetic problems. Ellen dreaded doing addition where everyone could see her, because she was so poor in arithmetic. At her desk she could at least put her hands in her lap and count quickly on her fingers.

She took her place at the blackboard. Otis took the space beside her. He picked up a long piece of chalk and squeaked it on the blackboard. Ellen put her hands over her ears.

"Otis, you are not co-operating," said Miss Joyce. "All right, class. We will start with an easy problem. Write these numbers in a column. Nine, four, seven."

Oh dear, thought Ellen. Sevens and nines were always hard. She drew her numbers slowly and very carefully to give herself time to think. Otis scribbled his figures, drew a long line under them, and wrote the total while Ellen was drawing a neat plus sign. She didn't mean to look at Otis's work but, somehow, she could not help turning her eyes toward it.

"Hey! You're peeking," said Otis in a loud whisper.

"I am not!" said Ellen, and quickly wrote her total. Even though she knew it was wrong, she wrote one hundred and thirty-seven.

Miss Joyce looked around the room. "Everyone look at Ellen's work, please," she said. "Ellen has made a mistake that is very easy to make if we are not thinking. Ellen has added nine and four correctly. That gave her thirteen. Then, instead of adding seven to thirteen, she put the seven at the end of thirteen. That gave her one hundred and thirty-seven instead of the correct answer. Who can give me the correct answer?"

"Twenty," said Linda loudly, and looked triumphantly at Ellen. Linda always seemed to be right when Ellen was wrong.

"That's right, Linda. I am sure Ellen knew better. She just wasn't thinking." Miss Joyce smiled reassuringly, but Ellen didn't feel any better. She would never get to clap erasers by making silly mistakes in arithmetic.

"All right, boys and girls. Erase your work."

Everyone grabbed for an eraser. There were never enough erasers to go around, but for once Ellen managed to snatch one. So did Otis.

"Miss Joyce," said Linda from the front blackboard, "we have only two erasers here and they have more than their share at the side board."

"Who will be kind and give an eraser to the front blackboard?" asked Miss Joyce.

Ellen disliked giving up her eraser, especially since it would mean sharing one with Otis. It wasn't often that she had an eraser all to herself. But, to please Miss Joyce, she took her eraser to the front blackboard and handed it to Linda.

"Thank you, Ellen. You are a good neighbor." Miss Joyce smiled at Ellen. "Ready for the next problem."

Ellen hoped she had pleased Miss Joyce enough to be chosen to clap erasers, but when recess came, Miss Joyce selected George and Linda. Ellen was terribly disappointed. Surely there must be something she could do to please Miss Joyce.

"Why don't you bring something to school?" suggested Austine sympathetically. "Then maybe Miss Joyce would choose you."

Ellen thought this was a good idea. All the boys and girls in Ellen's room liked to bring things to school to show the class. The next morning Ellen brought an autumn leaf which she thought was unusually pretty. Joanne brought a larger and more colorful leaf, so no one paid much attention to Ellen's leaf.

A few days later Miss Joyce was reading a chapter about plants out of *Science Reader, Book Three*. She explained that many plants lived only one season. These plants were called annuals. The class could think of lots of annuals they had seen. They named petunias, pansies, zinnias, and many others.

Then Miss Joyce explained that perennials were plants that grew year after year. Amelia said that the roses and pinks growing in her yard were perennial, because they had been there as long as she could remember.

Austine waved her hand and said that geraniums were perennials.

"They are not," said Linda, without even raising her hand. "They don't count, because they grow in pots."

"They do not! In California . . ." Austine glanced at Ellen and continued. "Where I used to live they grow for years and years. They grew in our yard and they were higher than the fence."

Miss Joyce smiled. "Austine is right, Linda. Geraniums are perennials, even though we cannot grow them outdoors in winter in Oregon."

Miss Joyce went on to explain that biennials were plants that took two years to grow and produce seed. The class thought and thought, but no one could think of even one biennial.

Finally Miss Joyce said, "I can think of two very common biennials—beets and carrots. You probably have never seen a beet or a carrot that has grown a flower and seeds, because we eat them before they are that old."

Then Ellen remembered the beet she had seen

in a vacant lot several blocks from her house. It had been growing for months in a lot where someone had once had a vegetable garden. Ellen always looked for the beet when she went down that street, because it was the biggest beet she had ever seen. The last time she had looked, the stalk growing out of it was over two feet high. Now that she thought about it, the stalk did have a funny thing at the top. She supposed it was the beet flower, but it certainly wasn't very pretty.

Ellen raised her hand. "I know where there is a beet with a flower on top. If you want, I could bring it to school to show the class."

"Thank you, Ellen," said Miss Joyce. "I think that is an excellent idea. We do not often see a beet blossom. If the weather is unusually cold, the plants must be dug up and buried in pits and then replanted in the spring. However, we had such a mild winter last year that perhaps it wasn't necessary."

Ellen smiled happily. At last she had thought of something that would please Miss Joyce. Surely she would get to clap erasers if she brought a rare biennial beet flower to school.

Early the next morning Ellen ran up on Austine's porch out of the rain and in her rubber boots tap-danced, *hop, one-two-three.* This was the way the girls summoned each other instead of calling or ringing the doorbell. She waited and danced again. *Hop, one-two-three, slap down, slap down.*

Austine's brother Bruce came to the door. "Austine isn't ready," he said.

Then Austine came to the door in her stocking feet and with her hair uncombed.

"Oh, Austine. Couldn't you have been ready on time for once in your life?" Ellen asked. "I've just got to get that beet so Miss Joyce will like me."

"I tried to be early," replied Austine. "I can't help it if I broke both shoelaces and had to look all over for a pair of socks that matched."

Ellen sighed. "Well, I guess I'll see you at school then. I've got to hurry if I'm going to get over to the lot and pull that beet."

It was three blocks to the vacant lot. Running

made Ellen so warm that she unbuttoned her rain-coat, even though the rain was falling faster every minute. It was hard to run in her rubber boots, because they made her feet so heavy. And she had to hold the hood of her raincoat in place or the wind blew it off. As she ran, she began to be afraid the beet might be gone when she got there. It was such a big beet someone might have pulled it up and eaten it.

But when Ellen climbed up the bank of the vacant lot, the beet was still there. It was growing on the edge of the lot next to a white house. With her boots squshing in the mud, Ellen walked through the weeds. The beet was even larger than she had realized. The stalk was at least three feet high.

She took hold of the stem near the ground and tugged. Nothing happened. She examined the lower part of the stalk and saw that it was growing out of an immense beet. Part of it showed above the ground.

Ellen found a stick and scraped away some of

the dirt. She grasped the stalk and pulled again. The beet did not budge.

Ellen did not know what time it was, but she knew she must hurry. She found a bigger stick and dug away some more dirt from the vegetable.

She pulled again. The beet did not move.

Ellen was getting desperate. She decided to use her hands. They were already dirty from the beet stalk anyway, so she might as well get them dirtier. She would be very, very careful not to touch her dress. She squatted and began to claw the dirt away from the beet. The soil was cold and heavy. It stuck to her fingers. When she had uncovered half the beet, she saw that it was nearly six inches across.

Once more she grasped the stalk and pulled, bracing her feet. The beet began to come slowly out of the ground.

Just then a window in the house next door flew open and a woman's voice called out through the rain, "What are you doing, little girl?"

Ellen started. The long, thin taproot broke and

Ellen sat down in the mud with a thump. She had the beet in her hands!

"Pulling a beet," answered Ellen guiltily. It had not occurred to her that the beet might have an owner. She thought things growing in vacant lots belonged to everybody.

Sitting on the ground in the pouring rain and holding the precious vegetable, she asked timidly, "Is it your beet?"

"Yes, it is," said the woman crossly. "What do you want it for?"

"I want to take it to school to show the class how beet seeds grow," said Ellen politely, "but if it is your beet you may have it. I didn't know it belonged to anyone."

"No, I don't want it," snapped the woman. "It's too old and tough to eat. Take it, but after this, don't go pulling things up on other people's property!" She slammed the window.

Ellen felt bad, because she would not have touched the plant if she had thought it belonged to anyone. Holding the beet carefully so she wouldn't knock off any of the blossoms, she got up from the wet ground and twisted around to look at herself. The backs of her legs were muddy. Her raincoat, which she was outgrowing, was covered with mud. So was the bottom of her dress hanging below the raincoat. She found it useless to try to wipe off the mud, because her hands were even muddier than her clothes. Maybe she could wipe it off at school. Or maybe the rain would wash it off. She didn't have any time to waste.

It was not until Ellen was back on the sidewalk that she noticed how the broken beet root had smeared juice all over the front of her freshly starched dress, her pretty green one with yellow flowers printed on it. The red juice stood out in ugly contrast. Oh dear, she thought, what if it doesn't wash out? What will Mother say?

Ellen had never been tardy in her life. Now she ran as fast as she could through the downpour in her heavy boots. Even though her starched dress wilted, she could not take time to put down her beet and button her raincoat. Her hood blew back as soon as she pulled it in place. She tried to hold the dirty vegetable away from her clothes, but that made running more difficult.

Finally she decided she was already so dirty that more dirt couldn't make any difference. She clutched the beet against herself with both hands and ran faster, her boots clumping on the sidewalk and her raincoat flying out behind. When her hood blew off again, she gave up trying to keep it in place. Her hair whipped around her face in wet strings.

She was still several blocks from school when she heard the first bell ring. I'll never make it, she thought. I'll be tardy and Miss Joyce won't like it. I've just got to run faster.

"Hey! Where do you think you're going?" Ellen heard someone call. Without stopping, she looked around and saw Bruce, Austine's big brother, riding his bicycle along the curb beside her.

"To—school," she gasped.

"What are you doing with that beet?"

"Miss Joyce—wants me—to—bring it." Ellen

slowed down. She was so out of breath she couldn't run another step. "I guess I'm going to have to be tardy."

Bruce looked disgusted. "Oh, come on," he said. "I'll give you a lift. You can sit in the basket."

"Would you?" asked Ellen gratefully.

"Sure. Here, let me hold your beet while you climb up."

"Be careful. Don't break the stalk." Ellen stepped up on the front tire of the bicycle and scrambled into the basket. It was not very comfortable and her feet stuck out awkwardly. Bruce handed her the beet and began to pedal.

Ellen found it exciting to ride in the basket with the rain in her face. When Bruce steered the bicycle by turning the handle bars, he stee Ellen, too. Ellen hoped it wouldn't tip over held her beet in one hand and grasped th of the basket with the other.

Wet and dirty though she was, Ellen cretly pleased. None of the other girls eve to school in the bicycle basket of an eighth-grad

boy. Ellen was glad he was wearing his boy scout uniform under his raincoat. He looked so hand-some in his uniform.

They reached Rosemont School just as the last boys and girls were straggling into the building.

"Look at Ellen!" shouted Linda. A group of girls from Miss Joyce's room paused to watch.

Bruce held the beet while Ellen climbed down ⬛ of the basket. As she jumped from the bicycle, ⬛m of her dress caught on the wire basket ⬛re.

⬛my," said Ellen, as she looked at the tear. ⬛ such a pretty dress and now it was spoiled. ⬛ would her mother say?

⬛Here, take your old beet," said Bruce, who did

not enjoy having a lot of third-grade girls staring at him. "I haven't got all day."

"Thanks a lot, Bruce," said Ellen shyly.

"Aw, that's all right. Now I've done my good deed for the day," said Bruce, and pedaled off to the bicycle racks.

"Broth-er! Are you a mess!" yelled Otis cheerfully, when he saw Ellen. "When Miss Joyce sees you, I bet she sends you home!"

Such a thought had not occurred to Ellen. "She will not send me home," she answered, but her voice quavered. Otis was probably right. She was so wet and muddy Miss Joyce would send her home to change her clothes. Then she would not get to show her beet to the class and would never get to clap erasers.

Otis, who never cared about being tardy, splashed through the rain to Ellen. "You tore your dress," he announced.

"I know it," said Ellen crossly.

Otis began to chant loudly, "I see London, I see France, I see somebody's under . . ."

Ellen clutched her raincoat around her and shouted, "Otis Spofford, you keep quiet!" Then she burst into tears.

"I see London, I see France, I see somebody's . . ."

"Otis Spofford, you shut up this very instant!" It was Austine. She ran splashing through the puddles. "Come on, Ellen," she said, taking her by the arm. "I'll help you get cleaned up."

"But it's time for the second b-bell," said Ellen, as she tried to wipe her eyes with the back of one muddy hand. "You'll be tardy."

"No, I won't," said Austine. "When I saw you might be late, I asked Miss Joyce if I could go help you get the beet and she said I could. Come on."

"I see London, I see France," sang Otis. "I see . . ."

"Otis Spofford! You mind your own business," snapped Austine. "Ellen is my best friend and I won't have you picking on her!"

CHAPTER THREE

Leave It
to Otis

SOAP, water, and lots of paper towels removed much of the mud from Ellen. "I'm beginning to look cleaner," she said, "but what shall I do about this awful tear in my skirt and this beet juice? It won't wash off."

Austine thought a while. "I know," she said. "You keep on scrubbing. I'll be back in a minute."

She returned with a roll of Scotch tape that she always kept in her pencil box and her extra sweater. Quickly she tore off pieces of tape and stuck Ellen's dress together.

"There. That ought to hold if you don't move around too much. Mother always says just about anything can be mended with Scotch tape or a hairpin." Austine gave Ellen's skirt a final pat. "Now put on my sweater and button it all the way down the front."

Ellen's fingers were so cold she could hardly push the buttons through the holes. "Your sweater is awfully big on me," she said, thinking how lucky she was to have Austine for her best friend. And they really were best friends now. Austine had said so herself.

"That's better," said Austine. "You stand by the radiator for a while and dry off some more."

"I guess I am pretty wet," said Ellen. "How do I look?" she asked anxiously.

Austine studied her critically. "Well, you don't look as good as you did when you started for school, but at least your collar is pretty clean and my sweater is so long on you, it covers up a lot of the beet juice. You look better than you did a little while ago."

"You don't think Miss Joyce will send me home, do you?" Ellen tried to smooth some of the wrinkles out of her skirt. "Otis said she would."

"I don't think so," said Austine. "When you sit at your desk, the dirt will hardly show at all. Don't pay any attention to that old Otis Spofford. He just thinks he's smart."

Ellen tried to fluff out her hair with her fingers. "Maybe we better not stay here any longer. Miss Joyce might send someone to look for us." She picked up her beet.

"That's the biggest beet I've ever seen," whispered Austine, as they walked quietly through the empty halls to their room. "I know Miss Joyce will ask you to clap erasers now."

Miss Joyce was listening to part of the class recite from the *Away We Go* reader at a circle of chairs in the front of the room. The boys and girls were taking turns reading aloud slowly and with expression. Ellen tiptoed across the room and laid her precious beet on the teacher's desk. Miss Joyce nodded and smiled at her.

Then Ellen quickly slipped into her seat, so her muddy skirt wouldn't show. She took her arithmetic workbook out of her desk and started to

work her problems for the day. Miss Joyce had
smiled, so she must be pleased. Now Ellen would
surely get to clap erasers. And not only that; she
would also get to tell the class about her biennial
beet during science period. Ellen could hardly
wait.

She glanced at the plant on Miss Joyce's desk.
She hoped some of the other children were looking at it, too. It was such a big beet. Probably
no one in the room had ever seen such a big beet
before. And just think, it had taken two whole
years for the plant to grow that flower. Why, when
that beet was a seed, Ellen was a little girl in the
first grade.

Ellen looked around to see if anyone else was
admiring her beet. George, who sat in front of
her, was looking at something, but it was not her
beet. He was leaning across the aisle, staring at
something on Otis's desk.

Ellen looked too. She saw four small brown
objects, about the size of peas. They were rolling
from side to side. Ellen couldn't imagine what

they were or what made them move. As she watched, one of the brown objects hopped.

By this time some of the other boys and girls were staring at Otis's desk.

"What are they?" whispered George.

Otis did not answer. He swept the objects into the palm of his hand and watched them rock back and forth. Ellen still couldn't understand what made them move. Otis was not moving them. He held his hand still. Then he put them back on his desk. The things continued to rock.

Ellen, leaning farther out of her seat to watch

the mysterious things, accidentally knocked her arithmetic workbook on the floor. The noise made Miss Joyce look up, and all the boys and girls who had been watching Otis were instantly busy with their arithmetic. Otis was busiest of all.

Ellen hastily picked up her workbook. Goodness, she had better be more careful. Miss Joyce certainly wouldn't send her out to clap erasers if she interrupted the lesson. However, the teacher did not say anything, but went on with the reading.

In a few minutes Otis was playing with the little brown objects again.

"Aw, come on, Otis. What are they?" whispered George once more.

"Wouldn't you like to know?" answered Otis.

Ellen couldn't keep still any longer. "What makes them move?" she whispered.

"I see London, I see France," murmured Otis, as he watched the little brown objects in his hand.

"You do not!" said Ellen, and quickly returned to her arithmetic.

Linda, who sat in front of Otis, turned around to watch. "I know what they are," she boasted.

Just then the little group noticed that the reading circle in the front of the room had stopped reciting. Miss Joyce had closed her book and was watching Otis and the boys and girls who sat near him.

"Otis, what do you have in your hand?" Miss Joyce asked.

"Nothing," answered Otis. Miss Joyce looked at him, but did not speak. "Aw, just some Mexican jumping beans," he admitted.

"I'm sure all the boys and girls are interested in your jumping beans, Otis," said Miss Joyce, "but instead of interrupting our lessons by playing with them, I think it would be much nicer if you showed them to the class during our science lesson."

"I know what makes them jump," said Linda eagerly, without even raising her hand. "It's a little worm . . ."

"Never mind, Linda," interrupted Miss Joyce.

"Otis will tell us about the jumping beans during the science lesson. Put them in your pocket until this afternoon, Otis." Then Miss Joyce went on with the reading lesson.

Ellen and Austine exchanged worried glances. They both knew everyone would rather hear about jumping beans that came from far-off Mexico and jumped all by themselves than about Ellen's beet, which just grew in a vacant lot a few blocks from school and didn't do anything.

That old Otis Spofford, thought Ellen. He would have to bring his jumping beans to school today. Why couldn't he have brought them yesterday or tomorrow? And after I worked so hard to bring the beet to show Miss Joyce. It's just like Otis. If I had brought jumping beans to school, he'd probably walk in leading a kangaroo or something. Now Miss Joyce is more interested in his beans than my beet. He'll probably get to clap erasers, and he's already clapped them three times since school started. It just isn't fair.

Ellen found she could not keep her mind on

her arithmetic. After a while she saw Otis slip his hand in his pocket and take out his jumping beans again. He put them on the seat beside him and watched them roll back and forth. Ellen couldn't help watching.

"Otis Spofford!" said Miss Joyce suddenly. "If I have to tell you once more to put those Mexican jumping beans back in your pocket, I shall have to take them away from you."

"Yes, Miss Joyce," said Otis.

Ellen was secretly pleased, but she wished Miss Joyce had said Otis would not get to tell about his beans. She didn't know what she would do if Miss Joyce forgot all about her beet. Maybe she could remind her somehow.

Then Miss Joyce dismissed the *Away We Go* readers, and they took their seats. She went to the section of the blackboard that was reserved for the class's daily news. At the top was printed "Our News." Under that Miss Joyce printed the date. Ellen watched her chalk move across the blackboard. "Today is Thursday," she wrote. "It is raining." Then she asked, "Has anyone any suggestions for news?"

After glancing anxiously at Ellen, Austine waved her hand so frantically that Miss Joyce could not help seeing her. "You could put down that Ellen brought a beet," said Austine.

"That is a splendid suggestion." Miss Joyce wrote, "Ellen brought a beet for our room."

Ellen and Austine exchanged a triumphant look. Again Ellen thought how lucky she was to have such a loyal girl for her best friend. Austine wouldn't let Miss Joyce forget about the beet if she could help it.

Otis waved his hand. "You could put that she sure got dirty bringing the beet." Ellen and Austine gave him a disgusted look.

Miss Joyce suggested, "Let's say it in a different way." She wrote, "Ellen worked very hard to bring the beet."

Ellen smiled modestly. She noticed that Austine was whispering to Amelia and wondered what they were saying.

Miss Joyce said, "We have room for one more sentence. Has anyone any suggestions?"

Amelia raised her hand and said, "You could say that Ellen is going to tell us about the beet when we study plants today."

Miss Joyce wrote the sentence on the blackboard while Amelia and Austine smiled at Ellen. So that was what they were whispering about! Ellen might have known her best friend would think of something like that.

Now Ellen knew that at last she had pleased Miss Joyce. Hadn't she written on the blackboard that Ellen had worked hard to bring the beet and that she was going to tell the class about it? Surely Miss Joyce would reward such a hard worker by choosing her to clap erasers.

All through social studies and arithmetic and lunch period Ellen waited anxiously for afternoon recess. When the class went to the blackboard to do spelling, she wrote her words over and over as fast as she could, just so she could erase them and be sure that one eraser was good and dirty.

Finally the time came. When Miss Joyce looked around the room, Ellen held her breath. She didn't know what she would do if Miss Joyce didn't choose her. "Let's see," said the teacher. "Who will take the erasers out to clean them during recess? Ellen, you may take half of them."

Ellen let out her breath in a sigh of relief. At last Miss Joyce had chosen her to clap erasers! Now she knew Miss Joyce liked her as much as she liked the other boys and girls.

Then Miss Joyce said, "Otis, you may take the rest of the erasers."

Oh dear, thought Ellen in dismay, anybody but Otis. It was just her luck to have to clap erasers with Otis after waiting so long. She just knew Otis would do something to spoil everything. He always did. He was that kind of boy.

"Yes, Miss Joyce," said Otis, dropping three of his jumping beans on the floor. With a guilty look, he quickly leaned over to pick them up.

"I am sorry, Otis," said Miss Joyce. "You are not co-operating. You were supposed to keep your

Mexican jumping beans in your pocket until our science period. Bring them to me and I will keep them in my desk until after school."

"Aw," muttered Otis as he gathered up his beans and handed them to Miss Joyce.

"And I think you had better stay in during recess," said the teacher. "Austine, you may clap erasers instead of Otis."

Ellen beamed across the room at Austine. Not only was she going to clap erasers, she was going to clap them with her best friend! And if Miss Joyce kept Otis's jumping beans until after school, he wouldn't get to talk about them during science period after all.

Joyfully Ellen gathered her half of the erasers from the chalk rail. On her way out of the room, she hesitated near Miss Joyce, who was standing in the doorway.

"Thank you for choosing me," she said shyly. "I've always wanted to clap erasers."

"You have?" Miss Joyce sounded surprised. "Why, if I had known that, I would have let you

take them sooner. I haven't asked you before because cleaning erasers is such dirty work and you always keep your dresses so clean."

Ellen hurried out of the building with Austine, and they clapped erasers furiously. As clouds of chalk dust blew out into the rain, Ellen coughed. "Austine, do you know what?" she asked happily between coughs. "Miss Joyce liked me all the time!"

CHAPTER FOUR

Ellen Rides Again

THE arrival of spring meant different things to different people. To Mrs. Tebbits it meant spring cleaning. To Mrs. Allen it meant planting seeds and setting out new flowers. To Ellen and Austine spring meant something much more important. It meant no more winter underwear.

The two girls were walking home from the library one warm spring afternoon. They felt light and carefree in their summer underwear. It was a wonderful feeling. It made them want to do something exciting.

At the library Austine had been lucky enough to find two horse books. "I wish I could ride a horse sometime," she said.

"Haven't you ever ridden a horse?" asked Ellen.

"No. Have you?" Austine sounded impressed.

"Oh, yes," said Ellen casually. "Several times."

It was true. She had ridden several times. If she had ridden twice she would have said a couple of times. Three was several times, so she had told the truth.

"Where? What was it like? Tell me about it," begged Austine.

"Oh, different places." That was also true. She had ridden at the beach. Her father had rented a horse for an hour and had let Ellen ride behind him with her arms around his waist. The horse's back had been slippery and she had bounced harder than was comfortable, but she had managed to hang on.

And she had ridden at Uncle Fred's farm. Uncle Fred had lifted her up onto the back of his old plow horse, Lady, and led her twice around the barnyard. Lady didn't bounce her at all.

And then there was that other time when her father had paid a dime so she could ride a pony

around in a circle inside a fence. It hadn't been very exciting. The pony seemed tired, but Ellen had pretended it was galloping madly. Yes, it all added up to several times.

"Why haven't you told me you could ride?" Austine demanded. "What kind of saddle do you use?" Austine knew all about different kinds of saddles, because she read so many horse books.

"Oh, any kind," said Ellen, who did not know one saddle from another. "Once I rode bareback." That was true, because Lady had no saddle.

"Golly," said Austine. "Bareback!"

Ellen was beginning to feel uncomfortable. She

had not meant to mislead Austine. She really did not know how it all started.

"Oh, Ellen, you have all the luck," exclaimed Austine. "Imagine being able to ride horseback. And even bareback, too."

"Oh, it's nothing," said Ellen, wishing Austine would forget the whole thing.

But the next day at school Austine did not forget about Ellen's horseback riding. She told Linda and Amelia about it. They told Barbara and George. Barbara and George told other boys and girls. Each time the story was told, it grew.

Even Otis was impressed and he was a difficult boy to impress. When the girls started home after school, he was waiting on the edge of the school grounds. He had a piece of chalk and was busy changing a sign from "Bicycle riding forbidden at all times" to "Bicycle riding bidden at all times." Otis crossed out "for" every time he had a chance, but the rain always washed away the chalk marks.

"Hello, Ellen," he said, walking along beside her in his cowboy boots. Since Christmas Otis had

worn boots instead of Oxfords. He was not wearing spurs today. Miss Joyce had asked him not
to wear them to school.

Ellen and Austine ignored him.

Otis kicked at the grass along the edge of the
sidewalk. "Say, Ellen, is it true you ride a lot?
Even bareback?"

"Of course it's true," said Austine.

"I wish people would stop talking about it," said
Ellen crossly. "What's so wonderful about riding
a horse, for goodness' sake?"

"Gee whiz," said Otis enviously. "Some people
have all the luck."

The girls continued to ignore him. He followed
them for a while, kicking at the grass, and then
turned down another street.

When the girls came to Austine's house, they
found Mrs. Allen on her knees beside a flat box
of pansy plants. She was taking them out of the
box and setting them into a border along the
driveway.

"Hello there," she said. "Since tomorrow is

Memorial Day and there isn't any school, how would you like to go on a picnic?"

Ellen did not say anything. She thought Mrs. Allen meant her, too, but she was not sure. She hoped so. That was the trouble with the word *you*. Sometimes it meant one person and sometimes it meant a lot of people. Maybe Mrs. Allen was talking to Austine and not to both of them.

Mrs. Allen said, "Ellen, I have already asked your mother and she says you may go."

"Thank you. I'd love to go." Maybe a picnic would make Austine forget about horses. And if they went on a picnic, Austine couldn't come to Ellen's house to play and perhaps say something about horseback riding in front of Mrs. Tebbits. Ellen was worried about what her mother would say if she found out how Ellen had exaggerated.

"Where are we going?" asked Austine.

"We're going to drive out toward Mount Hood. The rhododendrons are beginning to bloom, and I thought it would be nice to see them blooming in the woods."

The next morning at ten o'clock Ellen ran down Tillamook Street and around the corner to Austine's house. For her share of the picnic she carried eight deviled eggs carefully packed in a cardboard box. Mr. Allen was backing out the car. Mrs. Allen sat in the front seat and Austine in the back.

"Hop in," said Mr. Allen. "Bruce isn't going with us. The boy scouts are marching in a parade."

Ellen was glad she and Austine could each sit by a window. That made it easier to look for white horses and to play the alphabet game. The first one to see a white horse got to make a wish. Ellen was going to wish Austine would forget about her horseback riding.

The girls always played the alphabet game when they rode in a car. Each watched the signs on her own side of the road for the letters of the alphabet. Each letter had to be found in order or it did not count. The k in a Sky Chief Gasoline sign could not be used unless a j had already been seen. The girl who had a Burma Shave sign on her side of the road at the right time was lucky because it contained in the right order both u and v, two hard letters to find. The game went quickly at first, because there were lots of signs, but as they neared the mountains the signs became more scarce.

Ellen was looking for a Texaco filling station for an x when Austine shouted, "Look, a white horse! I've got dibs on it." She shut her eyes to wish.

Ellen was sorry she had not seen the horse first. She needed a wish. Finally both girls were down to z. By then the car was winding along the mountain roads.

"Z!" shouted Ellen. "I win. There was a sign by that bridge that said 'Zigzag River.' "

"That's all right," said Austine generously. "I'm going to get my wish."

It was a few more miles along the highway that Austine saw the horses. "Look, Daddy! Horses for rent, fifty cents an hour! Please stop," she begged.

Mr. Allen drew over to the side of the road near some horses in a makeshift corral. Austine scrambled out of the car and ran to the horses, while the others followed.

"Daddy, please let us go horseback riding. All my life I've wanted to ride a horse. Please, Daddy. You and Mother could go on and look at the rhododendrons and come back for us."

"Would it be safe for the girls to ride alone?" Mrs. Allen asked the man with the horses.

"Please, Mother," begged Austine. "Make my wish come true."

"Sure. Kids do it all the time," answered the man. "They ride up that dirt road as far as the old sawmill and turn around and come back. The horses know the way. Takes about half an hour. Road runs right along the highway."

"They won't be thrown from the horses?" asked Mrs. Allen.

"From these horses?" said the man. "No, lady. These horses worked at a riding academy for years."

"You're sure they're gentle?"

"Yes, ma'am. Gentle as kittens."

"The girls could hang onto the saddle horns," suggested Mr. Allen.

"Oh, Daddy, you aren't supposed to hang onto the saddle horn. Only tenderfoots, I mean tenderfeet, do that. We'll be safe, because Ellen has ridden a lot and I know all about riding from books."

Ellen wished Austine would keep still. She was not at all sure she wanted to ride, especially without a grownup along.

"I suppose it would be safe to let the girls ride for half an hour," said Mrs. Allen. "We could walk along the dirt road and look at the rhododendrons while they rode. That way they would be within shouting distance."

"All right, girls, which horses do you want to ride?" asked Mr. Allen, taking a handful of change out of his pocket.

Ellen thought she had better act brave even if she didn't feel that way. "The spotted horse is nice, but I think I'd rather have the brown one over in the corner of the pen." She thought the brown horse looked gentle.

"I'll take the pinto on this side of the corral," said Austine, glancing at Ellen.

Oh dear, thought Ellen. I've said the wrong thing. I wish I'd read some horse books.

Austine watched eagerly and Ellen watched uneasily while the man saddled and bridled the two horses. "O.K., kids," he said.

Ellen walked over to the brown horse and patted him gingerly. He seemed awfully big when she stood beside him. But he looked down at her with large gentle eyes, and Ellen felt braver.

The man held out his hand, palm up.

Oh, I wonder if he wants me to give him some money, thought Ellen. It must be that, but I'm sure Austine's father paid him. Or maybe he wants to shake hands. A sort of farewell.

"Come on, girlie. Step up," said the man. "Don't be scared. Brownie isn't going to hurt you."

My goodness, thought Ellen. I guess he expects me to step in his hand. I suppose it's all right. His hand is dirty anyway.

She put her foot into his hand and he boosted

her onto the horse. The ground seemed a long way below her. And Ellen had forgotten how wide a horse was. The man shortened her stirrups and then helped Austine onto the pinto. Ellen patted Brownie on the neck. She was anxious to have him like her. If only she had a lump of sugar in her pocket.

"Look," cried Austine. "I'm really on a horse."

Ellen knew she was expected to take the lead. "Giddap," she said uncertainly. Brownie did not move.

The man gave each horse a light slap on the rump. They walked out of the corral and ambled down the dirt road as if they were used to going that way. Austine's mother and father followed on foot.

Ellen carefully held one rein in each hand. As she looked at the ground so far below, she hoped Brownie wouldn't decide to run.

"I'm going to call my horse Old Paint like in the song," said Austine, who never missed the Montana Wranglers on the radio and knew all about cowboy songs. "I wish I'd worn my cowboy neckerchief."

"Yes," said Ellen briefly. She didn't feel like making conversation.

When Austine's horse moved in front, Ellen took hold of the saddle horn. It wasn't so much that she was scared, she told herself. She just didn't want to take unnecessary chances.

"I wish we'd worn our pedal pushers," said Austine. "It's sort of hard to feel like a cowgirl in a dress."

"I wish we had, too."

Maybe this wasn't going to be so bad after all. The horses seemed to know the way, and Ellen found the rocking motion and the squeak of the saddle rather pleasant. She was even able to look around at the trees and enjoy the woodsy smell.

Then when they had gone around a bend in the road, Brownie decided it was time to go back to the corral. He turned around and started walking in the direction from which they had come.

"Hey," said Ellen anxiously. She pulled on the

right rein, but Brownie kept on going. "Stop!" she ordered, more loudly this time.

"What are you going that way for?" asked Austine, turning in her saddle.

"Because the horse wants to," said Ellen crossly.

"Well, turn him around."

"I can't," said Ellen. "He won't steer."

Austine turned Old Paint and drew up beside Ellen. "Don't you know you're supposed to hold both reins in one hand?" Austine was scornful.

Ellen didn't know. "I just held them this way to try to turn him," she said. She took them in her left hand. They were so long she wound them around her hand.

Austine leaned over and took hold of Brownie's bridle with one hand. "Come on, Old Paint," she said, and turned her horse forward again. Brownie followed.

"Thanks," said Ellen. "My, you're brave."

"Oh, that's nothing," said Austine modestly. "You don't steer a horse," she added gently. "You guide him."

"Oh . . . I forgot." Ellen wondered how she would ever explain her ignorance to Austine. What would her best friend think when she found out how Ellen had misled her?

The horses plodded on down the woodsy road. Through the trees the girls could see the highway and hear cars passing. Austine's mother and father appeared around the bend, and Ellen began to feel brave again.

"Let's gallop," suggested Austine.

Ellen's legs were beginning to ache. "How do you make them gallop?"

"Dig your heels in," said Austine.

"Oh, I wouldn't want to hurt the horse," said Ellen.

"You won't hurt him, silly. Cowboys wear spurs, don't they?"

Ellen timidly prodded Brownie with her heels. Brownie ambled on.

Austine dug in her heels. Old Paint began to trot. At first Austine bounced, but soon she rode smoothly. Then her horse began to gallop.

When Old Paint galloped, Brownie began to trot. Ellen began to bounce. She hung onto the saddle horn as hard as she could. Still she bounced. Slap-slap-slap. Her bare legs began to hurt from rubbing against the leather of the saddle flap. Slap-slap-slap. Goodness, I sound awful, she thought. I hope Austine doesn't hear me slapping this way.

Austine's horse, after galloping a few yards, slowed down to a walk. "Whoa, Old Paint," cried Austine anyway, and pulled on the reins. Old Paint stopped and Austine panted a minute.

"I did it, Ellen!" she called. "It was just a few steps, but I really, truly galloped. I hung on with my knees and galloped just like in the movies."

"Wh-wh-oa-oa!" Ellen's voice was jarred out between bounces. Brownie trotted on. Slap-slap-slap.

Austine began to laugh. "I can see trees between you and the saddle every time you go up. Oh, Ellen, you look so funny!"

Slap-slap-slap. Ellen didn't think she could

stand much more bouncing. It was worse than being spanked.

"Ellen Tebbits! I don't think you know a thing about horseback riding."

"Wh-wh-oa-oa!" When Brownie reached Old Paint he stopped. After Ellen got her breath, she gasped, "I do, too. It's just that the other horses I rode were tamer."

The horses walked on until the road curved down to the edge of a stream.

"Oh, look. There's a bridge," exclaimed Ellen, looking up.

"I guess the highway crosses to the other side of the stream," said Austine. "I wonder if the poor horses are thirsty."

There was no doubt about Brownie's wanting a drink. He left the road and picked his way down the rocky bank to the water.

"Poor horsie, you were thirsty," said Ellen, patting his neck.

But Brownie did not stop at the edge of the stream. He waded out into it.

"Whoa," yelled Ellen, above the rush of the water. "Austine, help!"

Brownie waded on.

"Austine! What'll I do? He's going swimming!"

"Here, Brownie! Here, Brownie!" called Austine from the bank. Her voice sounded faint across the surging water.

When Brownie had picked his way around the boulders to the middle of the stream, he stopped and looked around.

"Look, he's in over his knees!" Ellen looked down at the swirling water. "Giddap, Brownie!"

"Kick him in the ribs," yelled Austine from across the stream.

"I don't want to hurt him," called Ellen, but she did kick him gently. Brownie did not appear to notice.

"Slap him on the behind with the ends of the reins," directed Austine from the bank.

Ellen slapped. Brownie turned his head and looked at her reproachfully.

By this time some hikers had stopped on the

bridge. Looking down at Ellen, they laughed and pointed. Ellen wished they would go away.

Brownie lowered his head to drink. Because Ellen had the reins wound around her hand, she could not let go. As she was pulled forward, the saddle horn poked her in the stomach.

"Oof," she said. Hanging over the horse's neck, she clung to his mane with one hand while she unwound her other hand.

Brownie looked at her with water dripping from his chin. Ellen thought it was his chin. Maybe on a horse it was called something else.

Austine broke a branch from a huckleberry bush that grew out of an old log at the edge of the stream. She waved it toward Brownie. "Here, horsie. Nice horsie."

Brownie glanced at her with mild interest.

"Oh, go on, Brownie," said Ellen in disgust. She kicked him hard this time. Brownie looked at her sadly and swished his tail.

A couple of cars stopped on the bridge and the occupants looked down at Ellen and laughed.

"Yippee!" yelled one of the hikers and everyone laughed. "Ride 'em, cowboy!"

"Do something, Austine," Ellen called across the water. "Our half hour must be nearly up."

"Maybe I could ride back and get the man who owns the horses," Austine yelled back.

"No, Austine. Don't leave me here alone," begged Ellen. "Maybe I could get off and wade. I don't think the water would come up to my shoulders."

"The current's too strong," called Austine. "And anyway, we're supposed to bring the horses back. You can't go off and leave Brownie."

Austine was right. Ellen knew that she couldn't leave Brownie. She might lose him, and the man would probably make her pay for him. At least, she thought he would. She had never heard of anyone losing a horse, so she wasn't sure. "I can't stay here forever," she called.

"Mother and Daddy should catch up with us in a minute," Austine called. "They'll know what to do."

That was just what was worrying Ellen. She didn't want the Allens to see her in such a predicament. What would they think after Austine had told them she had ridden before? Maybe they had wandered off to look at rhododendrons and were lost in the woods by now.

Still Brownie did not move. Ellen wondered what it would be like to try to sleep on a horse. Again she wished she had brought some lumps of sugar. She could have eaten them herself when she became hungry.

One of the hikers climbed down the bank to the edge of the water. "Need some help, little girl?" he called.

"Oh yes, please," answered Ellen gratefully.

Jumping from boulder to boulder, the man drew near her, but he could not get close enough to reach Brownie's bridle. "Throw me the reins, little girl," he directed.

Ellen threw them as hard as she could. They fell into the water, but the man grabbed them as the current carried them toward him.

"Come on, old fellow," he said, pulling at the reins. Meekly Brownie began to pick his way around the boulders toward the bank.

"Oh, thank you," said Ellen, when they reached dry ground. "I guess I would have had to stay out there all day if you hadn't come for me."

"That's all right," said the man. "The trouble is, you let the horse know you were afraid of him. Let the old nag know you're boss and you won't have any trouble."

"Thank you, I'll try," said Ellen, taking a firm grip on the reins. "Good-by."

Just then Austine's mother and father appeared around the bend in the road. "Enjoying your ride, girls?" asked Mr. Allen.

"Oh yes," said Austine. "We just stopped to give the horses a drink."

"It's time to turn back now," said Mrs. Allen.

"All right, Mother," said Austine.

The girls headed their horses toward the corral. Ellen was so embarrassed she didn't know quite what to say to Austine. What would Austine think of her after this? What would she tell the kids at school?

Finally, when Austine's mother and father were a safe distance behind, Ellen said in a low voice, "I guess I didn't know quite as much about horseback riding as I thought I did."

"Your horse was just hard to manage, that's all," said Austine generously.

"Austine?" said Ellen timidly.

"What?"

"You won't tell anybody, will you? You won't tell that Otis Spofford what happened, will you?"

Austine smiled at her. "Of course I won't tell. We're best friends, aren't we? It'll be a secret like the underwear. Giddap, Old Paint."

"Thank you, Austine," said Ellen gratefully. "You're a wonderful friend. And you know what? I'm going to look for some horse books the next time we go to the library."

The horses, knowing they were headed toward hay, showed more spirit. Ellen held the reins firmly. That Brownie was going to know who was boss. She began to enjoy herself. She pretended she was returning to a ranch after a hard day riding the range.

"I didn't know horses had such long hair," she remarked.

"It's their winter coat," explained Austine. "They'll shed it this summer."

Ellen laughed. "Just like winter underwear," she said.

CHAPTER FIVE

The Twins

ONE morning early in August Ellen roller-skated to Austine's house. It was a beautiful day and, as Ellen skated through the shadows of the maple trees, she thought about her wonderful idea. It was the best idea she had thought of in a long, long time. She could hardly wait to tell Austine about it.

Austine, who was already out on her skates, coasted toward Ellen. "Hi," she said. "Come on, let's practice skating backwards."

"I can't stay long today, Austine. Mother says I have to change my clothes after a while and go downtown with her to pick out patterns and materials, so she can start making me some new school clothes. I wish I didn't have to go. I'd rather skate."

"I suppose Mother will take me down sometime before school starts and get me some boughten dresses," said Austine.

"Austine, you know what?" Ellen twirled her skate key around by its string. "I have the most wonderful idea!"

"Oh, Ellen, tell me!"

"Well," said Ellen, "wouldn't it be fun if we could have dresses alike? And go downtown together Wednesday, when I go to show the dentist the bands on my teeth, and pick out our very own material and pattern all by ourselves?"

"Oh, Ellen," squealed Austine. "That's a wonderful idea!"

"People might even think we were twins," added Ellen.

"Of course, we don't look a bit alike," said the practical Austine, "but they might think we're the kind of twins who don't look alike." She thought a minute and said, "The trouble is, your mother makes your dresses and my mother buys mine."

"Doesn't your mother ever sew?" asked Ellen. She couldn't imagine a mother not knowing how to sew.

"Well, sort of. She mends things and she lets my dresses down when they get too short. Maybe she could make a dress if I asked her to. Maybe it would be safer to ask your mother first," suggested Austine. "If she says you can, then maybe Mother will let me."

This seemed like a good idea. If one mother said yes, the other usually did too. The girls were always careful to ask the right mother first. Now they skated back to Ellen's house, clumped up the front steps on their skates, and called to Mrs. Tebbits through the screen door. Ellen explained what they wanted to do.

"Well, I don't know," said Mrs. Tebbits, putting down her dustcloth and coming to the door. "Are you sure you would wear the dresses after they were made?"

"Oh yes, Mother. We want people to think we're twins. They might think we were the kind that don't look alike. Please, Mother, say we can."

Mrs. Tebbits smiled. "I suppose you'll have to learn to choose your own clothes sometime. If Mrs. Allen says you may, it's all right with me."

"Oh, thank you," said both the girls. Then they clumped down the steps, skated back to Austine's house, clumped up her front steps, and called through the screen door.

Mrs. Allen laughed when she heard what they wanted. "Where do you girls get such ideas?"

"Please, Mother," begged Austine. "Ellen's mother says we may."

"But, Austine," protested her mother, "I always buy your dresses ready-made. You know what my sewing is like."

"We'd pick out a real easy pattern," promised Austine. "Please, Mother, couldn't you make me a dress just once?"

Mrs. Allen smiled. "All right, dear. Since you want it so much, I'll make you a dress."

On Wednesday, after the dentist had looked at the bands on Ellen's teeth, the girls rode the escalators, which were more fun than elevators, to the fifth floor of a department store. Ellen led the way to the pattern department, where she had shopped with her mother many times. The girls knew they wanted a dress with a flared skirt, so it did not take them long to select a pattern.

Choosing the material came next. The two mothers had agreed that the girls could buy anything they wanted as long as it did not cost more than seventy-nine cents a yard. There was so much to choose from: plain materials, plaids, polka dots, stripes; materials printed with leaves, flowers, kittens, ducks, airplanes—almost any design you could think of. The girls looked and looked.

Ellen felt the materials between her thumb and forefinger the way she had seen her mother feel yard goods. She was not sure how it was supposed to feel, but she liked to pretend she knew a good piece of material when she felt it.

"I don't want stripes," said Austine firmly. "Mother always chooses dresses for me with up-and-down stripes to make me look thinner."

Ellen giggled. "Mother thinks stripes running around make me look fatter. And I don't want a dress printed with kittens. I have kittens on my pajamas."

"I'd like something with red in it," said Austine. "Mother never buys me anything red."

"I like red, too," agreed Ellen. "Here's a piece with some red in it. Look, Austine, it's printed with darling little red monkeys."

"And palm trees," exclaimed Austine. "I like palm trees."

The girls admired the material. Red palm trees were printed on a white background. From each tree a small red monkey hung by its tail. Ellen and Austine thought it was the nicest material they

had ever seen and just what they wanted for their dresses.

For the next few weeks the girls talked of nothing but the first day of school, when they would dress alike. Austine even changed the part in her hair from the left side to the right side so she and Ellen would look more alike. They agreed that they would both wear white bobby socks. Since it would be their first day in the fourth grade, their mothers said they could wear their black slippers. After that they would have to wear their everyday Oxfords.

Mrs. Tebbits cut out Ellen's dress first. When it was ready to try on, Austine came over to watch. It fitted nicely, and Ellen twirled around in her flared skirt. Even though it was without a collar and sleeves and the skirt was not hemmed, the girls could see it was going to be a lovely dress.

"I wish Mother would hurry up with mine," said Austine.

But Mrs. Allen did not sew as quickly as Mrs. Tebbits. She pinned and basted and stopped frequently to read the directions. She spent a lot of time ripping. Sometimes she stuffed the whole thing in a drawer and did not sew at all for several days. The girls became more and more anxious. Ellen asked about the dress so many times she felt it would not be polite to ask any more. Austine stopped mentioning it altogether.

Then the evening before school started, Austine telephoned Ellen. "Guess what!" she said. "Mother is hemming my dress this very minute and it'll be ready in time for tomorrow. I thought she wasn't going to get it finished, but she worked all afternoon, and Bruce and I fixed dinner so she could sew. Don't forget to wear your white socks."

The next morning Ellen dressed carefully and did not squirm while her mother brushed her hair and tied her sash in a nice fat bow. She twirled around to admire the fullness of her skirt and peered over her shoulder at her sash. She liked her new dress more than any dress she had ever owned. She could hardly wait to walk into her new fourth-grade room with Austine.

She walked as quickly as she could to Austine's house. She walked, because her sash might come untied if she ran. She tap-danced, *hop, one-two-three,* on Austine's porch and waited for Austine to come out. She waited a long time. *Hop, one-two-three, slap down, slap down.*

Finally Austine came out with a piece of toast in her hand. "Well, come on," she said crossly.

Ellen stared. Austine's dress did not look the least bit like hers. The material was the same, but everything else was different. Austine's skirt sagged at the bottom. The sleeves did not puff the way Ellen's did and the collar did not quite meet under Austine's chin. The buttons were sewed on over snaps instead of buttoning through real buttonholes. The waist was too tight and gapped between the buttons. Worst of all, there was no sash to tie in a nice fat bow.

"But, Austine," said Ellen in dismay, "there's supposed to be a sash."

Austine finished the last bite of toast and licked her fingers. "Well, there isn't going to be on mine.

I'm bigger than you are, and Mother had to allow extra material on the sides of the dress. And then she made a mistake in cutting the sleeves, and when she got through there wasn't any material left for a sash. Mother says I'm too plump to wear such a wide sash, anyway."

"Oh. That's too bad." Ellen didn't know what to say. She was terribly disappointed. She supposed she ought to offer to take off her sash, but it was such a lovely one. Besides, her mother had stitched it to her dress at the sides, so she would not lose it.

"Well, I think you might take off your sash," said Austine, pulling a basting thread out of her hem. "We're supposed to look like twins, you know. It was all your idea in the first place."

"I can't take it off. It's sewed to my dress," said Ellen, secretly glad she could not take off her sash.

Austine did not answer. The girls walked in unhappy silence. When they were half a block from school, the first bell rang.

"Come on," said Ellen, glad to have an excuse

to speak. "We'd better run." She started to run and as she did, Austine grabbed the end of her sash. The bow came untied. Austine laughed.

"Oh, Austine. Now look what you've done," said Ellen, trying to retie the bow. It was hard to tie a bow she could not see. One loop pointed up and the other pointed down. Austine did not offer to help.

Austine seemed to feel better after that. She even took Ellen's hand as they hurried down the hall to their new fourth-grade room. Ellen squeezed her hand in excitement. The first day in a new room was so exciting. She thought the boys and girls going into the third-grade room looked very young.

In the fourth-grade room the children were busy deciding which seats to sit in.

"What are you dressed that way for?" demanded Linda Mulford, as some of the class crowded around the two girls.

"Maybe they think they're dressed like twins," said Joanne.

"Girls always want to be twins," said George. "I think it's dumb."

"Where's your sash, Austine?" asked Amelia.

"I don't see why everyone has to make such a fuss, just because we happen to have dresses made out of the same material," said Ellen.

Otis came over to inspect the dresses. "Look at the monkeys!" he yelled. Leaning forward and dangling his arms, he bent his knees and walked like a monkey.

"Cut it out, Otis," ordered Austine. "You think you're funny, but you're not!"

Otis scratched himself under one arm and pretended to look for fleas.

"Don't pay any attention to him," said Ellen, and turned her back.

Otis hopped around in front of her and scratched himself under the other arm.

"Oh!" said Ellen furiously, and whirled around again.

Then Mrs. Gitler, their new teacher, came into the room and asked the boys and girls to take seats.

When Ellen started to hurry to a back seat, Austine took hold of her sash and, as Ellen walked, it came untied.

"Austine, I wish you'd stop untying my sash," snapped Ellen.

"I didn't untie it," said Austine. "I held on to it and you untied it when you walked."

Ellen was so cross she didn't answer. By that time all the back seats were taken, so she chose a seat by the window. Austine took a seat by the blackboard. Ellen was sorry Austine didn't want to sit beside her any more. She really didn't want to quarrel with her best friend.

It was not until lunch time that the real trouble began. When the class crowded into line at the door to wait for the bell to ring, Ellen knew that Otis and Austine were standing behind her. "Hey, quit shoving," she heard Otis say.

Someone bumped against Ellen. "Excuse me," said Austine, and then added to someone else, "Well, you don't have to push. There's plenty of room."

It's silly, getting mad over a sash, thought Ellen. I'm going to pretend nothing has happened. She was about to turn around and ask Austine to eat lunch with her in the cafeteria, when she felt someone grab her sash and yank.

This time Ellen was really angry with Austine. Without stopping to think, she whirled around with her hand out. She turned so quickly that Austine, who was laughing, didn't have time to dodge. Before Ellen realized what was happening, the palm of her hand struck Austine's face with an angry smack. Austine gasped and put her hand to her cheek. Her face turned red and her eyes filled with tears.

Ellen stared, horrified. The classroom began to buzz with whispers. Mrs. Gitler clapped her hands. "Boys and girls, I don't like this talking. If I hear any more, we shall all go back to our seats until we can be quiet."

Ellen had slapped her best friend. How could she have done such a terrible thing? She was so shocked she could not speak.

CHAPTER SIX

The Substitute Rat

WHEN the bell rang, the class filed into the hall. Embarrassed and ashamed, Ellen walked to the cafeteria and bought her lunch. She knew everyone was talking about her. With flaming cheeks she carried her tray to a corner table and ate alone. It did not take her long to finish her lunch. She was not hungry.

She returned to her new fourth-grade room, took her reader out of her desk, and started to read straight through it. After the first page she sat twisting her hair and thinking. The more Ellen thought, the more unhappy she became.

What bothered her most was the question of who should apologize first. Should she tell Austine she was sorry or should Austine tell her she was sorry? Of course, slapping someone was worse than untying a sash, but just the same, if Austine had left Ellen's sash alone, she would not have had her face slapped. Yes, it was Austine who really started it. Ellen decided Austine should apologize first. Ellen would smile encouragingly at her and give her every chance to say she was sorry. Then Ellen would say she had not really meant to slap her at all, and they would be best friends again.

Now was the time to start. Ellen went outdoors and found Austine and Linda playing hopscotch. She walked slowly past the girls, but they were

having so much fun they didn't notice her. At least
Ellen thought they didn't notice her.

Austine leaned forward and threw her pebble
into a square. "And I was going to have a party
and invite her, but I'm not now," she said to Linda.

"I don't blame you a bit," said Linda. "She
thinks she's smart just because her dress is nicer
than yours."

It was no use. When Ellen went home from
school that day she changed her clothes and put
the monkey dress behind all the other dresses in
her closet. She hoped her mother would forget it.
Then she sat on the front steps, just in case Austine
might decide to come over to say she was sorry.
The shadows of the maple trees grew longer and
longer and still there was no sign of Austine.
When Ellen finally went into the house, she listened for Austine's *hop, one-two-three* and
dreaded going to school the next day. She was
practically an outcast, a terrible person who had
slapped her best friend, even if it was the best
friend's fault. If only she could begin her life

over again some place where no one knew her.

"Mother, do I have to go to Rosemont School?" she asked. "Couldn't I go to Glenwood?"

"No, of course not, dear," answered her mother. "We don't live in the Glenwood district. And you wouldn't want to go to Glenwood when all your friends are at Rosemont, would you? Whatever put such an idea into your head?"

"Oh, nothing," said Ellen, wondering if she had any friends.

The next day Ellen wore a blue dress to school. Austine appeared in a blouse and skirt. Whenever Ellen tried to catch Austine's eye to smile encouragingly, Austine was looking in another direction. When Joanne and Amelia invited Ellen to play hopscotch at recess, she felt a little better, but she couldn't help noticing how much Linda and Austine laughed over their game of hopscotch.

That afternoon after school Ellen walked to the library. On the way home she decided to go the long way past Austine's house. She really wanted to look at the gnomes on the lawn next door. She used to look at the gnomes before Austine lived there, and there wasn't any reason why she couldn't still look at them, was there? It would be nice if Austine happened to be in the yard and happened to speak to her, but of course that wasn't the real reason she was walking that way. She just wanted to look at the gnomes, that was all.

But Mrs. Allen, not Austine, was in the yard. "Why hello, Ellen," she said, and snipped another chrysanthemum. "We haven't seen you for a long time. Linda and Austine are in the kitchen baking brownies. Why don't you go in and help them?"

"Oh no, thank you. Mother is expecting me." Ellen hurried down the street. Why had she walked past Austine's house anyway? Now Mrs. Allen would tell Austine, who would think she had gone that way on purpose.

Then one morning the thing Ellen dreaded happened. Her mother asked her why she did not wear the dress with the monkeys and palm trees printed on it.

"I don't like the material so much after all," said

Ellen, "but I'd wear it if you could take off the sash. It—it keeps coming untied."

So Ellen wore the sashless monkey dress to school. She hoped Austine might notice the change and use it as an excuse to say she was sorry. Unfortunately, Otis was the only person who noticed. He walked like a monkey and scratched himself whenever he saw Ellen.

That was the day Mrs. Gitler announced that Rosemont was planning to hold open house, so that all the mothers and fathers could visit school. Each class would have its best work on exhibit, and children would be on hand in each room to answer questions. Others would entertain the parents. The little children's rhythm band would perform, the fifth- and sixth-graders would do folk dances in the gymnasium, and the seventh- and eighth-graders would serve cookies and coffee in the domestic-science room.

Some of the children from Miss Joyce's and Mrs. Gitler's rooms would give a play about the Pied Piper of Hamelin. That gave Ellen an idea.

If she and Austine were both in the play, Austine would have to speak to her. If they talked to each other in the play, it would be silly not to go on speaking out of the play, wouldn't it?

Then Mrs. Gitler explained that one of the eighth-grade girls would read aloud the story of the Pied Piper while the younger children acted and danced the story in pantomime. That would make the play much easier to give, because there would be no lines to memorize.

Ellen decided she still wanted to be in the play, even if there was no talking in it. It might give her a chance to be near Austine. Maybe she could help Austine with her dancing and they would become best friends again.

Mrs. Gitler said that George was to be the Lord Mayor. Ralph, Ronald, and Otis, if he would promise not to make trouble, were to be town councilmen. Then she read the list of boys and girls who were to be townspeople, those who were to be children, and those who were to be rats. Austine and Linda exchanged smiles when they learned they were both to be children in the play.

Ellen waited for Mrs. Gitler to read more names, but she said, "The rest of the boys and girls in the play will be from Miss Joyce's room."

Ellen was sure there must be some mistake. Maybe Mrs. Gitler had skipped her name or forgotten to put it on the list. At recess Ellen walked across the playground to her teacher. "Mrs. Gitler, did you forget to read my name?" she asked.

"I'm sorry, Ellen," answered Mrs. Gitler. "There weren't enough parts for everyone. Miss Joyce couldn't use any more townspeople or children, because they all do a Maypole dance at the end of the play when the Piper brings the children back, and there are only twenty-four streamers on the Maypole."

Ellen was puzzled. "My mother read me the story and it wasn't that way. The Piper didn't bring the children back."

"I know," said Mrs. Gitler, "but this is a creative play and we have changed the story so we can use the Maypole dance at the end."

It didn't seem right to Ellen to change a story out of a book just so there could be a Maypole dance, but she said hopefully, "I take dancing lessons."

"We can't use any more rats, because they dance in pairs," explained Mrs. Gitler. Then, seeing Ellen's look of disappointment, she said, "I teach the rats their dance, and I think it might be a good idea to have a substitute in case one of the rats is absent. How would you like to be a substitute rat?"

Ellen felt it was better to be a substitute rat than not to be a rat at all. "Would I get to practice?" she asked.

"You may watch rehearsals and if any of the rats is absent, you may take his place."

At least Ellen would be allowed to watch the others practice. She was sure that somehow she would make Austine notice her.

During the last period all the boys and girls who were to be in the play went to the auditorium. Miss Joyce took the children and townspeople up on the stage, while Mrs. Gitler gathered her rats on one side of the room to show them their dance. Ellen sat quietly on a folding chair to watch the dance of the rats. It was an easy dance that began with the rats skipping around in a circle holding one another's tails.

Otis, who was a town councilman and did not have to dance, wandered down from the stage. "What are you sitting there for?" he demanded of Ellen.

"I'm a substitute rat," said Ellen.

"Aw, whoever heard of a substitute rat?" said Otis, and laughed. "Substitute rat! That's good."

"Oh, you keep quiet," snapped Ellen.

"This is a dumb play," said Otis.

"It is not," said Ellen. "Mrs. Gitler says it's a creative play."

"What does that mean?" asked Otis. "No good?"

Ellen really did not know what creative meant, so she was glad Miss Joyce clapped her hands and said, "Everyone up on the stage. We'll go through the whole play from beginning to end without a narrator. All right, Grandmother Rat, take your place under the table. Now, children, enter from the left and remember you are supposed to be laughing and playing."

The children skipped out to the center of the stage. Austine was holding Linda's hand. Ellen thought they looked as if they were having lots of fun, as they smiled at one another and hippity-hopped around the stage. She felt lonely sitting all by herself.

"All right, Mayor and Town Council. Now you come in, and remember you are proud and haughty," directed Miss Joyce.

George and Otis and the rest of the boys walked around the stage with their noses in the air. After the children bowed to them, they sat at a table at the side of the stage.

"Hey, quit kicking me," said the grandmother rat, who was crouched under the table. Then she crawled out, skipped across the stage, and beckoned to the rest of the rats, who ran out to the center of the stage and went through their rat dance.

"Hup, two, three, four. Hup, two, three, four," counted Otis in a loud whisper.

"Otis, you are not co-operating," said Miss Joyce quietly, so she would not interrupt the rat dance. "And town councilmen do not put their feet on the table. Don't forget, you are supposed to be dignified."

The rats finished their dance and knelt at one side of the stage. Then the townspeople entered and shook their fists at the town council. "Remember, you are angry," said Miss Joyce. "You are angry because the town council has done nothing to get rid of the rats in Hamelin Town." The townspeople shook their fists harder and scowled.

When the Pied Piper appeared and bargained with the town council to get rid of the rats, Ellen stopped watching and looked at Linda and Austine instead. They were sitting on a pile of folded chairs at the side of the stage. Ellen wondered what they were whispering and giggling about. Maybe they were laughing because she was just a substitute rat. If only one of the real rats would be absent. Then she could be on the stage with Austine, instead of sitting on a hard folding chair.

The days before open house at Rosemont School were busy ones. The fourth-graders tried to make their room more attractive than any other. They brought plants from home and worked hard to keep their workbooks neat. And of course the "Pied Piper" cast rehearsed almost every day. Once a rat was absent and Ellen practiced the dance, but most of the time she sat, a lonely substitute rat, and watched Linda and Austine. The more they laughed and hippity-hopped, the lonelier Ellen felt. As the folding chair grew harder and harder, she almost wished she were not even a substitute rat.

The evening of open house it seemed strange to Ellen to be going into the lighted school building at night with her mother and father. She took them to the fourth-grade room and, as she hung her coat in the cloakroom, she wondered if Austine was getting ready for the play.

Then Ellen showed her mother and father her

desk. While she was explaining her arithmetic workbook, Linda and Austine came into the room. They were both wearing full purple skirts, white blouses, and black bodices that laced up the front. Ellen noticed they were wearing lipstick. They looked happy and important as they took a box of Kleenex from Mrs. Gitler's desk and hurried out of the room. Ellen looked wistfully after them. How rosy their lips looked and how pale she felt beside them.

Then Otis came into the room in his town councilman costume. He was wearing a blue jacket and what looked like long red cotton stockings and red bloomers. The stockings bagged at the knees and hung in folds around his ankles. "Hey, Substitute Rat," he said. "Mrs. Gitler wants you."

"What for?" asked Ellen, staring at Otis's costume. What could Mrs. Gitler want her for? To run an errand? Ellen was almost afraid to hope, but maybe Mrs. Gitler needed her to be a rat.

"How should I know?" said Otis. "Come on."

Ellen followed Otis to the classroom that was

being used for a dressing room. The children and townspeople were racing around in a game of tag. The rats in their brown suits were jumping over the seats. Miss Joyce clapped her hands from time to time, but no one paid any attention. Mrs. Gitler's cheeks were red, and her hair hung in wisps around her face.

"Did you want me, Mrs. Gitler?" shouted Ellen.

"Stand still, Lord Mayor, until I fix your crown." Mrs. Gitler took a tuck in the crown with a paper clip. "Yes, Ellen. We are short one rat. Joanne hasn't come, so you may put on her costume. Hurry, we haven't much time."

"Oh, thank you," said Ellen. She was a real rat at last! She found the costume and got into it, snapping it up the front after she had stuffed her skirt inside. She pulled the head of the suit over her hair, and then put on the rat mask, firmly tying the string at the back of her head. The eyeholes were too far apart and she couldn't see very well. She ran her hands over the mask and stroked her whiskers. Then she put one hand on a desk and the

other on the back of a seat and swung herself across. It felt wonderful to be a rat.

Now if she could only manage to be close to Austine! Ellen adjusted her rat face so her left eye could see out of the left hole in the mask. She was just starting across the room toward Austine, when something held her back. She turned and peered out of her mask.

"Otis Spofford!" she snapped, her voice muffled by her mask, which had no hole for her mouth. "You let go my tail." She snatched her tail from him.

Mrs. Gitler blew a whistle. "All right, boys and girls! Line up as you appear in the play. Children first, then the mayor and town council. Rats next. Quietly, boys and girls."

The children tiptoed along the hall to the back of the stage in the auditorium. Ellen heard the rhythm band finish "March of the Teddy Bears." She had a shivery feeling in her stomach when she heard the narrator read, "Hamelin Town's in Brunswick by famous Hanover City," and heard the curtains part.

"All right, children," whispered Mrs. Gitler, guiding them through an opening in the scenery. Ellen could hear the piano and the sound of the children's feet on the stage as they danced. Then the Lord Mayor and town council went on. Ellen moved her mask again so she could see through the left eyehole.

Now it was time for Ellen and the rest of the rats to scamper onto the stage. Ellen had watched the dance so many times she had no trouble following. She did get out of step when another rat stepped on her tail and once, when her mask slipped, she bumped into the rat in front of her. She tried to find her mother and father in the audience, but in no time at all the dance ended. The rats knelt on one side of the stage to watch the Pied Piper bargain with the town council. Ellen knew the Lord Mayor's money bag really contained pieces of chalk instead of gold.

Then the Piper held his pipe to his lips and pretended to play a tune. The rats scampered across the stage and off to the other side. Ellen's part in the play was finished.

Miss Joyce put her finger to her lips and whispered, "Rats, wait here as quietly as mice, so that you can take a bow at the end of the play." When the Pied Piper led the children of Hamelin Town off the stage, Miss Joyce told them to wait too. There were so many people crowded into the small space that Ellen began to feel uncomfortably warm in her flannel rat suit.

When she tried to lift her mask for a breath of air, she discovered that the string was tied in a hard knot. Oh well, she thought, it will be only a little while. Just the Maypole dance, and then it will be over. She heard Austine's voice nearby. Linda answered, and Ellen tried to hear what they were saying. She thought she caught the sound of her own name. Maybe Austine was telling Linda she wished she and Ellen had not quarreled. If only Ellen could find out. She wiggled through the rats and into the midst of the crowd of children, where she stood near Austine and tried to catch what she was saying.

Miss Joyce said in a loud whisper, "All right, children. Skip onto the stage and pick up your streamers. Try to keep your spaces even when you dance."

The first thing Ellen knew, she was pushed along with the children. "Hey!" she said, but her voice was muffled. "I'm not a child. I'm a rat!" She tried to squirm away, but everyone was pushing against her.

Ellen, the rat, was on the stage! She heard the audience laugh. Her mask was pushed out of place, so all she could see out of the left eyehole was the top of the Maypole. She tried to adjust it with one hand and grope her way off the stage with the other. Someone bumped into her and the mask slipped again.

The audience shouted with laughter. They must be laughing at me, thought Ellen. Whoever heard of a rat at a Maypole dance? She could hear the shuffle of the dancers' feet as they skipped up to the Maypole and back again.

"Beat it," whispered someone who was skipping past her.

Every time Ellen tried to fix her mask, someone bumped into her. And every time someone bumped into her, the audience laughed harder. She could tell by the sound of feet that everyone was skipping to the right in time to the music. She decided the best thing for her to do was skip to

the right too. She started to skip and found herself tangled in a Maypole streamer.

The audience gasped. "You get out of here," whispered the owner of the streamer, as he tried to untangle Ellen. "You made the pole tip."

Oh dear, thought Ellen. What if I had tipped over the Maypole! Now everyone was skipping to the left to unwind the tangled streamers. Ellen skipped to the left. By then everyone was going to the right again. Skip to the right, skip to the left. Would she never find her way out?

This time she skipped too far to the left. She bumped into the velvet curtain at the side of the stage. The audience howled. Oh my, she thought, I must be near the edge. What if I fell off? Hastily she skipped toward the back of the stage and promptly bumped into a piece of scenery. She felt it wobble and heard the audience shriek with laughter. "Bravo!" someone shouted.

Oh dear, she thought, it's almost time to weave in and out around the Maypole. If I don't get out of here I really will be tangled up. What will Mrs.

Gitler say if I spoil it all? Ellen gave a desperate tug at her mask. Still she could not get it off.

After someone stepped on her tail again, she grabbed it in her left hand and started skipping. Again she bumped into a streamer. The audience gasped. Someone said, "Look out, it's tipping!" The gasp ended in a sigh of relief, and Ellen knew the pole was upright again.

Just then someone grabbed her by the hand and hissed, "Skip!"

Ellen skipped. It was Austine who was holding her by the right hand. Austine was helping her out. Even though she could not see where she was going, Ellen was able to follow the dance, with Austine to guide her.

In and out they skipped. Ellen felt lighthearted. She and Austine were friends again! Through the eyehole of her mask she could see the top of the Maypole where the streamers were weaving a pattern. She was not spoiling the dance after all.

Austine was out of breath. "Listen," she panted in a whisper, "when I say stop, you'll be by the exit. I'll let go of your hand and you feel your way out."

"O.K.," agreed Ellen in a muffled whisper. Austine was such a wonderful friend.

Around they skipped. Ellen was alert for her order.

"Stop!" whispered Austine, and let go of Ellen's hand.

Instantly Ellen obeyed. She dropped her tail and groped with both hands. Sure enough, there was an opening in the scenery. She was off the stage at last! Even though the Maypole dance had not ended, the audience was laughing and clapping. My goodness, could they be clapping for me? thought Ellen.

Then she heard Miss Joyce say, "Sh-h." She wiggled through the crowd of rats to get her to untie her mask, but the Maypole dance had ended and Miss Joyce was saying, "All right, rats. Walk out and bow to the audience."

Once more Ellen found herself pushed onto the stage. This time it was all right, because she was with rats, not Maypole dancers. She bowed with the others, and the audience applauded wildly. Then she shuffled off the stage and returned to the dressing room with the rest of the rats. She could hardly wait to see Austine now that they were friends. If only she could get her rat mask off.

Ellen heard Mrs. Gitler's voice and groped across the room to her. "I can't untie my mask," she said in a muffled voice. Mrs. Gitler began to work at the knot. Hurry, thought Ellen. I've just got to talk to Austine.

Then she heard Austine's voice. "Who do you suppose that silly rat was that got mixed up in the Maypole dance?"

Ellen gasped inside her mask. Austine did not know who it was she had helped! She wasn't trying to make up the quarrel at all. She was just being kind to a lost rat, that was all.

"I'll bet it was that Ellen Tebbits," said Linda. "She thinks she's such a good dancer, she probably wanted to be in the Maypole dance."

Ellen started to say, "Linda Mulford, I did not!" but she stopped. She wanted to hear Austine's answer.

"Oh, I don't think it was Ellen," said Austine. "If it was, I wouldn't have helped her. Not after slapping my face like she did. And you know what? I didn't even untie her old sash. Otis did. That's what makes me so mad."

"Honest?" said Linda in a shocked voice. "You never told me. I thought you untied it."

"Well, I didn't. We were all crowded together in line and I was the only one who saw Otis do it. And then I get the blame."

Ellen's thoughts were in such a whirl she did not hear the rest of the conversation. So that was it! No wonder Austine was so mad at her. Of course. Why hadn't she thought of that before? Austine and Otis had been standing right behind her that day. And Otis—well, everyone knew the kind of boy Otis was. Oh my, what would she do now?

When Mrs. Gitler finally undid the knot and

took off the mask, Ellen saw her mother and father in the doorway looking for her.

"Oh, there you are," said her mother. "We couldn't tell which rat you were. You all looked alike in your costumes."

"That was some rat that danced the Maypole dance." Mr. Tebbits laughed. "I wonder who it was."

"Oh, just somebody that got mixed up," said Ellen, as she slipped out of her rat suit.

CHAPTER SEVEN

Dusty
Erasers

WEEKS passed and still the girls did not speak. Now, instead of trying to be near Austine, Ellen avoided her. She knew she was the one who ought to say she was sorry, not Austine. But Ellen felt that after waiting so long she couldn't say she was sorry she had slapped Austine. She just couldn't. Besides, Austine shouldn't have untied her sash on the way to school in the first place. Maybe Otis hadn't really untied the sash anyway. Maybe Austine just said he did. If only she could ask Austine about it—but of course she couldn't do that. There was only one other person who would know for sure—Otis.

Much as Ellen disliked having anything to do

with Otis, she made up her mind to ask him the first time she saw him alone. Finding Otis by himself was not easy. If he wasn't staying after school for not co-operating, he was leading the other boys in breaking up the girls' games in the schoolyard.

Finally she caught him alone during recess. He was hanging by his knees from a bar, so Ellen turned her head upside down to speak to him. "Otis, I've just got to know something. Did you really untie my sash that day I thought Austine did?" she asked.

Otis dropped to his feet and looked innocently at Ellen. "Who, me?" he asked, his eyes big and round. Then he leaned toward her. Using three fingers he suddenly pushed up the end of his nose and pulled down his lower eyelids. "Ya-a-a!" he said.

"Oh!" Ellen turned in disgust. She might have known Otis wouldn't tell her anything. Of course he had untied her sash. Why did she ever think he hadn't?

As Ellen went into the school building, she thought that if a fairy should appear and give her one wish, she would wish that she and Austine were friends again. No, she wouldn't either. She wouldn't risk wasting a wish, the way people in fairy tales did—speaking without thinking and using their wish to fasten a sausage on the end of someone's nose or something just as silly. She would use her wish to wish for as many wishes as she wanted as long as she lived. Then she would wish that she and Austine were friends again. It was a good idea, but of course no fairy appeared.

Gradually the days grew shorter and the autumn leaves on the sidewalk deeper. The nights were chillier. Mrs. Tebbits took Ellen downtown to buy her a raincoat to replace the one she had outgrown.

Then one morning before Ellen was out of bed, Mrs. Tebbits came into her room and took her winter underwear out of a drawer.

"Mother!" wailed Ellen, sitting up in bed.

"Now, Ellen, I don t want any fussing."

"But, Mother . . ."

"Ellen, you heard what I said."

So Ellen was more miserable than ever when she went to school that morning.

Then something happened to change everything.

When the class had finished writing the spelling lesson on the blackboard, Mrs. Gitler said, "These erasers seem to be unusually dusty this morning. I'm afraid someone will have to go out and clean them."

Every pupil waved his hand. Clapping erasers

during class was much more fun than clapping
erasers during recess.

"Ellen, you may take half the erasers," said Mrs.
Gitler. Ellen was pleased. Then Mrs. Gitler said,
"Austine, you may take the rest."

Ellen felt her face turn red. A couple of girls
giggled. How could Ellen face Austine alone after
all these weeks? Whatever could she say and how
would Austine act? Ellen's thoughts raced as she
gathered her half of the erasers. Of course they

would have to leave the room together. Then maybe she could run out in front of the building instead of at the side, where everyone usually went to clap erasers. No, that would only make things worse. Maybe she could pretend to choke on chalk dust so she couldn't talk.

"You better look out or she'll untie your sash," whispered Otis, as Ellen passed his desk.

The girls left the room with their erasers and, looking straight ahead, walked stiffly down the hall. They stalked out of the building into the cold schoolyard, where they could see their breath hanging in clouds in the chilly air.

Ellen briskly began to clap erasers. Clouds of chalk dust mingled with her breath. Maybe now was the time to say she was sorry. If only she hadn't waited so long.

Ellen looked at Austine, who had turned her back to beat her share of the erasers. She could still hear Otis whispering, "You better look out or she'll untie your sash." Oh no, she won't, thought Ellen.

Suddenly Ellen was angry. She was angry because she had not guessed that it was Otis instead of Austine who untied her sash. She was angry because she had slapped Austine. She was angry because Austine had not explained what had really happened but, most of all, she was angry because she and Austine had not made up. The quarrel had lasted so long that Ellen supposed now they never would make up.

The longer Ellen looked at Austine's back, the madder she became. All right, if she wants to stay mad, she can for all I care, thought Ellen. So there!

Then Ellen noticed the end of Austine's narrow sash hanging below her sweater. She was so angry she acted without thinking. Dropping her erasers, she grabbed Austine's sash and yanked with all her strength. There was a ripping, tearing sound. The bow not only came untied but, to Ellen's horror, one end of the sash tore loose from the dress and hung limply in her hand.

Austine whirled and faced Ellen. Her cheeks were red and her eyes blazed.

Ellen was frightened. She wanted to run, but somehow she could not move. She looked at Austine and then stared in dismay at the jagged hole in her dress and the limp sash in her hand. What had she done now? What would Austine do to her?

Ellen knew she had to say something. They just couldn't stand there staring at each other all day. She gulped and blinked her eyes to keep back the tears. "I—I guess I tore your dress," she said, look-

ing at the ground. She waited for Austine to move or to speak, but Austine was silent.

Ellen took a deep breath. "I sort of expected you to . . . well . . . slap me," she said timidly, drawing an imaginary line on the ground with her toe. She almost hoped Austine *would* slap her. At least, she would feel better if they were even.

"I c-can't," said Austine, and sniffed.

Startled, Ellen looked up. Austine was crying! Ellen felt worse than ever. She had never seen Austine cry before.

"Austine," said Ellen anxiously, "I didn't really mean to slap you that time. I thought you'd duck when I turned around. I'm sorry." There! At last she had said it. She felt better already. She added apologetically, "Here's your sash."

Austine took it and sniffed again. "Th-thank you." She rubbed her eyes with the torn-off sash. "I guess I was so mad at you because I didn't even untie your sash. Otis did."

"I know," said Ellen. "I heard you tell Linda that night at the open house when I was in my rat suit. You didn't even know I heard. I felt awful because I had blamed you."

"I shouldn't have untied your sash in the first place," said Austine fairly. "I felt so awful that day, because your dress looked so nice and mine was so funny-looking. I guess my mother just doesn't sew as well as your mother."

"It's all my fault, because dressing like each other was my idea in the first place."

"No, it wasn't. It was just as much my fault as yours." Austine stuffed her sash into her pocket.

"I guess it was really both our faults," said Ellen. "I hope your dress can be fixed."

"That's all right. I can stick my sash on with Scotch tape." Austine paused. "Ellen, there's something I've just got to know. Maybe it isn't any of my business, but . . . did your mother make you put on your winter underwear?"

Ellen hesitated. She didn't know whether she should tell Austine or not.

Then Austine said, "My mother made me put mine on this morning."

Ellen immediately felt better. "Isn't it funny? Mother made me put mine on this morning, too. It feels all bunchy and awful."

The girls looked at each other and began to laugh. They laughed and beat their erasers together until they choked on chalk dust and had to stop to catch their breath.

"You know something?" gasped Ellen happily. "I was the rat you helped that night at open house."

Austine giggled. "Were you really? I knew it was a girl rat but I never guessed it was you. Now I'm glad I helped you."

The girls smiled at each other and began to beat their erasers again.

"Why don't you come home with me after school and make some brownies?" asked Austine. "I'll let you break the eggs this time," she added generously. "In brownies it doesn't matter if the whites get mixed up with the yolks."

"I'd love to," said Ellen. "I've missed baking brownies at your house."

Otis appeared in the door of the school building. "Hey, you!" he said. "Mrs. Gitler sent me out to see what happened to you. Gee whiz, does it take all day to clap a few little old erasers?"

"We're coming, you—you old pieface," answered Ellen, gathering up an armful of erasers.

"Yah, pieface!" said Austine.

"Pieface! Pieface!" yelled the girls. "Otis is a pieface!"

"Aw, cut it out," said Otis.

A window flew open. "What are you girls doing?" demanded the principal.

"Just clapping erasers," answered Austine.

"I don't want any more noise in the schoolyard during classes. Return to your room at once," ordered the principal, and slammed the window.

"Broth-er, are you going to catch it!" said Otis cheerfully, and walked like a monkey back into the school building.

"Come on, Austine," said Ellen. She didn't care if they did catch it. She didn't care what happened. She and Austine were best friends again.